NORTH
DAKOTA
NIGHT
DRAGONS

Here's what readers from around the country are saying about Johnathan Rand's *AMERICAN CHILLERS:*

"I just read Terrible Tractors of Texas, and it was great! I live in Texas, and that book totally freaked me out!"

-Sean P., age 9, Texas

"I love your books! Can you make more so I can read them?"

-Alexis B., age 8, Michigan

"Last week, two kids in the library got into a fight over one of your books. But I don't remember what book it was."

-Kylee R., age 9, Nebraska

"I read The Haunted Schoolhouse in three days, and I'm reading it again! What a great book."

-Craig F., age 12, Florida

"I got Invisible Iguanas of Illinois for my birthday, and it's awesome! Write another one about Illinois!"

-Nick L., age 11, Illinois

"My brother says you're afraid of the dark, which is silly. But my brother makes things up a lot. I love your books, though!"

-Hope S., age 9, California

"I love your books! Make a book and put my name in it. That would be sweet!"

-Mark P., age 10, Montana

"I'm writing to tell you that THE MICHIGAN MEGA-MONSTERS was the scariest book I've ever read!"

-Clare H., age 11, Michigan

"In class, we read FLORIDA FOG PHANTOMS. I had never read your books before, but now I'm going to read all of them!"

-Clark D., age 8, North Carolina

"Our school library has all of your books, but they're always checked out. I have to wait two weeks to get OGRES OF OHIO. Can't you do something about this?"

-Abigail W., age 12, Minnesota

"When we visited Chillermania!, me and my brother met you! Do you remember? Anyway, I bought DINOSAURS DESTROY DETROIT. It was great!"

-Carrie R., age 12, Ohio

"For school, we have to write to our favorite author. So I'm writing to you. If I get a letter back, my teacher says I can read it to the class. Can you send me a letter back? Not a long one, though. P.S. Everyone in my school loves your books!"

-Jim A., age 9, Arizona

"I LOVE AMERICAN CHILLERS!"

-Cassidy H., age 8, Missouri

"My mom is freaked out by the cover of POISONOUS PYTHONS PARALYZE PENNSYLVANIA. I told her if she really wanted to get freaked out, read the book! It's so scary I had to sleep with the light on!"

-Ally K., age 12, Tennessee

"Your books give me the chills! I really, really love them, but I don't know what one I like best."

-Jeff M., age 12, Utah

"I was read WISCONSIN WEREWOLVES, and now I'm freaked out, because I live in Wisconsin. I never knew we had werewolves."

-Angie T., age 9, Wisconsin

"I have every single AMERICAN CHILLER except VIRTUAL VAMPIRES OF VERMONT. I love all of them!"

-Cole H., age 11, Michigan

"The lady at the bookstore told me I should read NEBRASKA NIGHTCRAWLERS, so I did. I just finished it, and it was GREAT!"

-Stephen S., age 8, Oklahoma

"SOUTH CAROLINA SEA CREATURES is the best book in the whole world!"

-Ashlee L, age 11, Georgia

"I read your books every night!"

-Aaron. W, age 10, New York

"I love your books! When I read AMERICAN CHILLERS, it's like I'm part of the story!"

-Leroy N., age 8, Rhode Island

"KREEPY KLOWNS OF KALAMAZOO is my favorite. It was awesome! I did a book report about it, and I got an 'A'!

-Samantha T., age 10, Illinois

#19: North Dakota Night Dragons

Johnathan Rand

Ran

An AudioCraft Publishing, Inc. book

Book storage and warehouses provided by Chillermania!©
Indian River, Michigan

Warehouse security provided by:
Lily Munster and Scooby-Boo

American Chillers #19: North Dakota Night Dragons
ISBN 1-893699-88-9

Printed in USA

First Printing - October 2006

NORTH DAKOTA NIGHT DRAGONS

VISIT CHILLERMANIA!

WORLD HEADQUARTERS FOR BOOKS BY JOHNATHAN RAND!

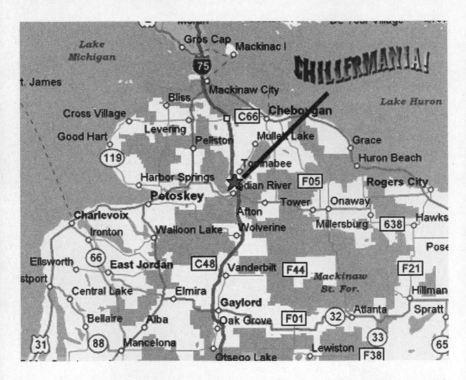

Visit the HOME for books by Johnathan Rand! Featuring books, hats, shirts, bookmarks and other cool stuff not available anywhere else in the world! Plus, watch the American Chillers website for news of special events and signings at *CHILLERMANIA!* with author Johnathan Rand! Located in northern lower Michigan, on I-75! Take exit 313 . . . then south 1 mile! For more info, call (231) 238-0338. And be afraid! Be veeeery afraaaaaaiiiid . . . .

1

Bismarck, North Dakota is known for several things. First of all, you probably already know that Bismarck is the state capitol. You might even know that Bismarck is the home of the Dakota Zoo, which is a lot of fun. Bismarck is North Dakota's 2nd largest city, named after Otto von Bismarck, who was Chancellor of Germany in the late 1800s.

Bismarck, however, is now known for something else:

Night Dragons.

That's right . . . Night Dragons. Oh, some people

don't believe they're real, just because they haven't seen them.

But if you ever come to Bismarck, and you go out at night, be warned:

Night Dragons are real.

They are as real as anything else . . . and just because some people haven't seen them doesn't mean they don't exist.

My name is Damon Richards, and I live on North 23rd Street in Bismarck. I've lived here only for a couple of years, because my dad gets transferred a lot, and we have to move. We've lived in a lot of cool places, but I really like Bismarck. I've made a lot of good friends.

The first time I saw a Night Dragon, I didn't think it was real. I thought I was dreaming. After all, if you saw a giant, winged creature slipping through the night sky, you'd probably think you were dreaming, too.

Now, however, I know better.

I remember that night very well. My friends and I had been outside playing a game called 'Kick the Can'. It's kind of a hide-and-seek game, and we play it a lot in the summer, usually around night time.

Well, we'd just finished our game, and everyone had gone home. The sun had set and it was dark.

I was on my way home. The place where we play is at the end of our street, so I was only a few blocks from where I live. At the end of our street is Lions Hillside Skate Park, which is a lot of fun. On the other side of the skate park, however, is St. Mary's cemetery. At night, it looks pretty spooky.

Streetlights lit up the pavement and the yards. I could see lights glowing in houses as I walked. Windows were open. I could hear a few television sets, their broken fragments of sound drifting through the warm evening. Crickets chirped. The air was damp and heavy, with the thick odor of recently mowed grass.

That's when I heard it.

A noise from above.

Oh, it wasn't a plane, that's for sure. And it didn't sound like a bat or a bird.

It was a whooshing sound: slow, and heavy, deliberate, like—

Wings.

I stopped and stared into the night sky. With all of the streetlights glowing like they were, it was hard to see, because the lights created a glare that clouded my vision.

Then, I heard it again: a heavy, whooshing sound, like air being pushed. I stared up into the sky, searching for whatever it was. After all, I was certain that the sound had come from above.

But I didn't hear anything more, and I didn't see anything out of the ordinary. Beneath a streetlight, a bat flitted and dove in silence, chasing a bug.

I was just about to start walking again . . . when I *did* see something.

Something in the sky.

Something *big*.

All I could see was its silhouette, a dark shadow. It swooped directly over me, turned, and sailed across the street and over a house.

And I couldn't be certain, but it looked like—

It landed!

Whatever it was, it landed in the yard behind the Kurtzner's house. Mr. and Mrs. Kurtzner are really nice. They're like my grandparents. Sometimes, Mrs. Kurtzner makes lemonade for all us kids on hot, summer days.

I looked behind me. The street was empty.

I looked all around. In a few homes, lights clicked off. People were settling in for the night. If I wasn't home in a few minutes, I would hear my mom calling out for me.

But I've still got a few minutes, I thought, looking into the dark yard where I'd watched the shadow go. *I could take a minute and see what the thing was.*

And so, I turned and walked across the lawn. I knew the Kurtzners wouldn't mind if I went into their back yard after dark. After all . . . I wasn't doing anything wrong. I just wanted to see what had landed in their yard.

Oh, I'd find out, all right . . . and I was just moments from being scared out of my mind.

2

As I approached the side of the house, darkness grew. Here, the streetlights faded. I looked up, and I could see stars sparkling across a black canopy. Several bushes grew tightly against the Kurtzner's house, and there were a few hidden crickets chirping.

I stopped where the back yard began and gazed into the murky darkness. I could see the silhouette of a large oak tree, and I could make out the faint form of a picnic table. However, I couldn't see anything else. It was just too dark.

Maybe if I get a little closer, I thought.

I have to admit, I was a little nervous. I wasn't sure what had made the strange whooshing sound. I wasn't sure what I'd seen. Yet, I was positive that, whatever it was, it had landed somewhere in the yard. In the tree, perhaps.

I took a step. The grass was squishy and soft beneath my feet. Somewhere, a dog barked. In the distance, a car horn honked.

I took another step. Then another, and another. Soon I was standing beneath the enormous tree. Here, beneath limbs thick with leaves, it was darkest of all. I looked up, but I couldn't see a thing.

This is silly, I thought. *I must be imagining things.*

I turned to walk home. It was only going to be a matter of minutes before Mom called for me, anyway. I looked forward to going to bed and reading my book. I was reading this really crazy story about fog phantoms in Florida. It wasn't true, but it was pretty freaky.

That's when I heard the noise. It was close by, but in the darkness, I couldn't tell where it came from. It was just a thin shuffling sound.

I looked up into the dark limbs. Even though my eyes had adjusted to the low light, I still couldn't make anything out. All I could see was darkness.

I listened . . . .

Nothing.

This is silly, I thought again. I was just about to walk away—

Suddenly, a long claw came from around the tree. Oh, I couldn't see it . . . but I sure could feel it! Sharp talons latched onto my shoulder, and I knew right then that I'd made a big mistake going into the Kurtzner's back yard.

3

You're probably thinking that I screamed.

Wrong.

I *howled*. I didn't know what had hold of me, but I howled as loud and long as I could . . . which didn't last, because the creature pushed me to the ground and tackled me!

"Wait a minute! Wait a minute!" I heard a girl's voice say. I stopped struggling as she drew away. "Who *are* you?" she asked in a huff.

"I could ask you the same thing!" I panted, trying to catch my breath. My heart was clanging in my chest, and I was gasping. The scare had really shaken me.

"No, who are *you?*" she repeated. "You're not Jason!"

"No, I'm not," I said. "I'm Damon Richards. Who are you?"

The girl stood, but it was still too dark to see anything but her shadowy figure. I, too, got to my feet, thankful it had been a girl . . . and not some weird creature.

"I'm Kamryn Kurtzner," she replied. "I thought you were my cousin, Jason."

"No," I said. "I live a few houses down."

"I'm really sorry," Kamryn said. "I thought you were my cousin, and I was trying to scare him. He's always trying to scare me like that, and I was just trying to get back at him. Man . . . you yelled really loud. Are you okay?"

"Yeah," I said. Then I laughed. "But you sure scared me. For a minute, anyway."

"What are you doing in my grandparents' back yard?" she asked.

"I . . . um . . . I thought I saw something," I replied.

"Like what?" Kamryn asked.

"I don't know," I said, gazing up into the star-filled sky. "I . . . I thought I saw something flying. Something big."

"You saw it, too?!?!" Kamryn asked. "I was standing on the back porch, looking for Jason, when I saw something swoop through the sky. It was too dark to see what it was. It was big, though. That's why I came out into the yard. I wanted to see what it was . . . and to scare my cousin."

"I thought I saw it land here in the yard," I said.

"No," Kamryn replied. "It swooped down low, but it didn't land. I think it—"

Suddenly, my mom's voice echoed from far down the street. *"Daaaaamon?!?!"* she called out.

I cupped my hands around my mouth. *"On my way, Mom!"* I shouted back. Then, I turned to Kamryn. I still couldn't see her in the darkness, so I had no idea what she looked like.

"I've got to go," I said. "Maybe I'll see you around."

"I'll be here for two weeks," Kamryn replied. "I'm from Michigan, but I'm staying with my grandparents. My cousin, Jason, is here, too."

"Have a good night," I said, and I turned.

"Sorry I scared you," Kamryn said again.

"No problem," I replied. I walked away, shaking my head.

Scared by a girl, I thought. *Sheesh.*

Of course, I had no way of knowing that I had something else in Bismarck to worry about.

Something that would scare me far worse than I'd already been.

Something that wasn't a girl.

Something that wasn't even *human.*

Something that was watching me at that very moment.

Watching me . . . and waiting.

I walked across the Kurtzner's yard and onto the sidewalk, comforted by the glowing streetlights. I've never really been afraid of the dark, but for some reason, I was glad I was on my way home. I was glad the claws that had grabbed me hadn't been claws at all . . . only Kamryn's hands.

But what had been in the sky? I wondered. I was certain I'd seen something fly over me. Something big. And I was sure it had flown over the Kurtzner's back yard. Maybe it hadn't landed, like I'd thought. I was sure I had seen something, though.

But, then again, maybe not. After all, it was very dark. With the streetlights on, it was difficult to see because of the glare. Maybe I hadn't seen anything at all.

But Kamryn had. She said she'd seen *something,* and she went into the back yard to see what it was.

What had she seen?

Probably nothing, I thought.

Up ahead, I could see our porch light glowing. Mom always left it on until I got home.

Suddenly, I noticed something.

I stopped walking.

My skin felt tingly all over, and I had a very strange feeling . . . like I was being watched.

I looked behind me, but there was nothing to see except houses, yards, and the ribbon of sidewalk as it snaked along the street. I heard a dog bark again, a long way off.

Then I heard the sound again. That heavy, deep whooshing sound, like wings.

Only this time, it was louder.

Closer.

Above me, not far above the streetlights.

I could almost see the dark shadow of something in the sky, circling.

Something big.

Wa-whoosh . . .

Something huge . . . .

Wa-whoosh . . . .

All of a sudden, an enormous dark figure dipped down and swooped beneath the streetlight. It was so big that it blocked out the light, and a shadow fell over me.

The fact that it was so big was frightening enough . . . but when I saw what it was, I knew my world was never going to be the same again . . . .

5

The creature was like nothing I'd ever seen before in my life.

Well, maybe not. I *had* seen creatures like this before, but they were in movies and comics and on the covers of books.

And yet, what I was seeing wasn't the cover of a book or a comic. It was straight out of the movies.

It was a dragon! It seemed impossible, but that's what it was!

He was deep, dark blue, with a long tail. His hind legs stretched out behind as he flew. His front claws were held forward, and it looked like he was holding something.

And his wings!

They were gigantic! The creature itself was as big as a car, but its massive wings were even bigger and wider. They thumped the air as the beast passed overhead.

His head turned from side to side, mouth open, tongue swirling. I saw rows of long, sharp teeth. His huge, glassy eyes looked fierce and menacing as he glanced from side to side and all around. I don't think he saw me, even though I was standing right below him.

A dragon? I thought. They aren't real! Dragons are only make-believe, from stories and movies!

Yet—

I was sure about what I'd seen. There was no way I could mistake it for an owl or anything else. It was just too big.

The dragon turned his head, like he was looking for something. He turned and circled beneath the light.

Suddenly, in the distance, I heard a throaty cry. It sounded angry. The dragon turned his head, and spewed a plume of fire from his mouth!

This isn't real, I thought. *I'm going to wake up any moment now, I just know it.*

But I didn't. I wasn't dreaming. I wasn't imagining. What was going on was real. There really was a dragon, circling in the sky above me.

Then, I heard another loud, animal-like shriek. It was as loud as a trumpet! Whatever it was, it was close . . . and getting closer by the second!

And when I saw what was making the sound, my knees turned to rubber. I sank to the grass, too terrified to even stand. All I could do was kneel and look up, my mouth open in disbelief.

Above me, in the sky, a horrifying black dragon was attacking the blue one!

The blue dragon whirled, narrowly escaping the gaping jaws of the black dragon. The black one, however, spun sideways and slammed into the side of the blue one.

Suddenly, an object was falling!

Whatever had been in the blue dragon's claws was falling . . . and it landed in the grass right beside me! I only glanced at it for a moment, just long enough to see what it was. It was all black, round, and about the size of a softball. It shone in the glow of the streetlight, reflecting the lamp with a pinprick of white.

I turned and looked up, just as one of the dragons coughed another plume of fire, sending a flame into the sky like a yellow geyser. The flame quickly burned out. There were several loud wails, but the dragons had risen above the light, and I could no longer see them.

I looked at the object laying in the grass. It appeared to be a stone of some sort. Then, I looked into the sky. The dragons were gone, and I couldn't hear a thing except the normal night sounds I heard every evening.

At the house across the street, a man had come to the front door and pushed it open. He looked around, then he looked at me. He scratched his head.

"Did you make that noise?" he asked.

I shook my head. "No," I replied.

"Then, what did?" he asked. He sounded a little mad.

"Dragons," I replied truthfully, and he stared at me. Then he shook his head, muttered something beneath his breath, and went back inside. The door closed behind him.

Again, I looked at the strange object in the grass. Then I moved closer, peering down at it. It was shiny and smooth, like a gemstone.

I wonder what it is? I thought. Again, I looked up and scoured the night sky. The dragons had vanished as quickly as they had arrived.

I turned my attention once again to the object in the grass. I leaned even closer, until I was only a few inches from it.

Then, I made a decision. After all, I was curious—and you would be, too.

I reached out my hand to touch the object. I didn't know it yet, but my whole world was about to change.

7

The moment I picked up the smooth, shiny object, there was an intense burst of light—like a giant eruption of lightning—all around me. It was so bright that I squinted and tried to drop the black ball . . . but I couldn't. It was like my whole body had tensed, and I couldn't relax my muscles. The light grew brighter and brighter, blinding . . . and then, it was gone.

I was still kneeling in the grass, trembling, holding the strange black object in my hand. I looked around at the houses and dark trees.

Something was missing.

What was it?

I peered into dark shadows. I looked up into shadowy tree limbs. Something was different, but I didn't know what it was. Everything seemed so strange, so oddly silent—

That's it! I thought. *There are no sounds! No crickets, no dogs barking, no horns honking in the distance!*

I slowly got to my feet, still carrying the black object in my hand. It was heavy and solid, and I was sure it was some sort of stone. I looked all around. Lights were on in homes, but I couldn't hear any sounds coming from them. No television voices, no laughter.

Nothing. Not a single sound could be heard.

However, when I looked across the street, I saw something I hadn't seen before.

A boy.

He was about my age. He was standing, motionless, near the side of a house.

"Hey," I called out to him. "Did you see that? Did you see the dragons and the bright light?"

The boy didn't move.

"Hello?" I called out again.

Still, the boy said nothing.

Strange.

I looked down the street. I knew I should get home, but I still had a few minutes. So, I began walking toward the boy.

"Can you hear me at all?" I asked as I drew closer to him.

He didn't say anything, nor did he move. In fact, as I got near, he remained so still he didn't even look real. He looked—

"Hey? Hello? Can you hear me?" I asked.

—*frozen.*

I stopped when I was right in front of him. The boy looked like one of those store dummies, the kind they use to model clothing.

Like a statue.

"Are . . . are you all right?" I asked.

The boy said nothing.

I was getting more and more freaked out by the moment. First, dragons showed up and got into a fight right above me. Then, there was the strange light when I touched the—

Wait a minute, I thought. I looked down at the black stone in my hand. *Does this have something to do with it? That flash of light happened the moment I touched the stone. What would happen if it touched someone else?*

I looked at the boy. I didn't recognize him.

I looked at the stone in my hand.

I raised it up and held it close to the boy's arm.

Closer . . . .

I touched the smooth stone to the boy's arm. There was a blinding flash of light, just like I'd experienced. The boy suddenly sprang to life . . . and began screaming in terror!

8

The boy was screaming so loud I almost started screaming myself. I leapt back, not knowing what he was going to do. Of course, he looked positively terrified of me.

"How did you get there?" he asked, after he'd stopped screaming. He was shaking right down to his shoes.

"I walked here," I said, pointing. "From over there. Near the street."

"I know where you *were*," the boy said. "I saw you kneeling in the grass. I thought something was wrong, so I was walking over to you. Now, all of a sudden, you're right in front of me! There was a bright flash of light, and you went from there to here!"

"I walked here," I repeated.

"That's bizarre," he said.

"What's bizarre," I said, "was that you were frozen. You didn't even move when I tried to talk to you. You started screaming when I touched you with this." I raised the stone so he could see it.

"What is it?" he asked.

"I think it's just a stone," I said. "The dragon dropped it."

The boy looked at me like I was from another planet. "The what?!?!" he exclaimed.

"You didn't see the dragons?" I asked.

"Are you crazy?" he replied, taking a step back.

"You . . . you didn't see them?" I asked.

He shook his head. "No," he answered. "I was looking for my cousin, Kamryn. I heard some strange noises in the sky, but I was on the other side of the house. When I came around this side, I didn't see anything or anyone but you."

"So, you must be Jason," I said.

The boy nodded. "You know Kamryn?"

"Sort of," I said. "I met her just a few minutes ago."

"I was hiding from her," Jason continued, "hoping to scare her when she came looking for me. When I came around the side of this house, I saw you kneeling in the grass. Then, in the very next second, you were standing in front of me. You freaked me out."

I thought about this for a moment. Nearly a full minute had gone by from the time I'd picked up the stone to the time I touched it against Jason's arm.

A full minute.

Where had that minute gone? I wondered.

But my wondering was going to have to wait. At that instant, there was a bloodcurdling screech from above.

"You had to have heard that!" I said.

"Yeah, I did," Jason replied, looking up into the inky sky. "What was it?"

There was no time to reply. Out of the dark night, a giant shadow emerged.

The black dragon!

Its mouth was open and its teeth were bared.

And he was diving down! He was attacking us!

Jason dove one way; I dove the other . . . and that's what saved us. The dragon hesitated, not knowing which one of us to go after, and that gave us just enough time to dart out of the way.

But not for long.

I could no longer see Jason. He was on the other side of the house, screaming like a crazed madman.

The dragon, however, had risen back into the sky. He had his eyes on me as I sprinted up the block, beneath the glowing streetlights. I was still carrying the black stone, and it never occurred to me that it might be what he was after.

I could hear the beast's wings pounding the air above me as I ran up the street, in the opposite direction of my house, back toward the park. The dragon was above me, over the treetops. He let out another screech, and I made a sudden left turn and darted into the shadows between two houses. Here, thick tree branches full of leaves provided a place to hide. I could no longer see the dragon, but I could hear him in the air, his leathery wings slapping madly as he wheeled through the night sky searching for me.

I huddled in the darkness between the houses and beneath the branches, where he couldn't see me. I could still hear his wings flapping furiously, and the thing was screeching like crazy. There was a sudden burst of lemony-yellow light, and through the frothy tree branches I saw a stream of flame arc across the sky.

What is happening?!?! I wondered. *What is going on?!?!*

I stayed close to the house, near a row of thick bushes. Nearby, I could make out the murky form of a large tree and a picnic table.

I'm back at the Kurtzner's house, I thought. *This is where Kamryn grabbed my shoulder and scared me.*

Suddenly, I saw a shadow running into the back yard. I was sure it was Jason. He was running to the back of his grandparents' house.

"Jason!" I yelled. *"Watch out! The dragon is above us, over the trees!"*

Problem was, Jason was in the back yard, and out in the open.

And the dragon knew it.

In a flurry of heavy wings and a wild, crazy screech, the dark creature hurled out of the sky, diving like a deranged eagle!

He was heading right at Jason!

10

I was about to shout to Jason again, but he'd heard the beast attacking from above. He made a quick dive, rolled, and leapt up . . . and just in time, too. Although I could only make out shadows, I could see the silhouette of the dragon as he swooped down at Jason, narrowly missing him. Jason tripped, tumbled, and rolled in the grass as the dragon turned and curled back into the sky. He was creating a lot of commotion, and I couldn't understand why no one was coming from the house . . . or, at least, coming to a window to see what was making all the ruckus outside.

The dragon was circling again, preparing for another attack, but Jason now had enough time to run for cover and get into the house. In fact, that's what I was planning to do, too.

Instead, Jason ran the other way, toward the big tree in the yard! All the while, the enormous dragon circled above, screeching and wailing.

"Jason!" I shouted. "What are you doing?!?! Get in the house!"

Jason shouted, but he wasn't talking to me.

"Kamryn!" he shrieked. "Kamryn! Come on! Come on! We've got to get inside!"

I peered through the darkness, struggling to see. Finally, I could make out the dark shape of Kamryn, standing near the tree. She wasn't moving.

Jason ran up to her. "Kamryn! Come on! We have to get in the house! Don't you see what's going on?!?!"

Kamryn didn't move.

I felt the weight of the black stone in my hand, remembering what had happened when I touched it to Jason's arm.

He was frozen, like a statue, I thought. *But when I touched the stone against his skin, he came to life. Maybe if I did the same with Kamryn . . . .*

I could see the dark silhouette of the dragon

circling above, and I could hear his heavy wings pummeling the air. Jason was still struggling with Kamryn, trying to get her to move.

I sprang, taking long strides across the dark lawn. It only took a couple of seconds to reach the pair, and I touched the stone against Kamryn's arm.

There was another flash of bright white light, and Kamryn came to life instantly. She was disoriented and confused, as you can imagine. She'd been frozen in time, like Jason. Now she was awake, and we were standing in front of her . . . with a vicious, bloodthirsty dragon in the sky, preparing for another attack.

"What . . . what's happening?!?!" Kamryn stammered. "Where did that flash of light come from?"

"No time to explain now!" Jason shouted. "Quick! We have to get into the house!"

We took off running through the yard, but the black dragon was already making another assault.

"Watch out!" I shrieked, and the three of us split off, heading in different directions. The dragon spewed a prong of fire, scorching the lawn and leaving thin blades of grass smoldering orange and red. It was so close to me that I could actually feel the heat against my skin.

Then, just as I thought we were going to make it, another dragon dropped out of the sky! This time, however, the beast didn't attack from above . . . he landed right in front of us, blocking our way into the house!

We were trapped!

Our situation seemed hopeless. There was a dragon in the sky, screeching and screaming . . . and another dragon had landed right in front of us!

The dragon before us was huge . . . every bit as big as the dragon in the sky. It was too dark to see anything but its shadow, but on its hind legs, the creature stood taller than the house!

Then, things began to happen so fast I couldn't even take time to question them. Things that, normally, I never would have believed. Things that weren't supposed to happen.

Then again, I wasn't sure *I* believed what was going on. Dragons? *Real* dragons? No way. I *had* to be dreaming.

And yet, I knew that if we didn't act fast, it was going to be the end of the road for the three of us . . . whether we were dreaming or not.

First, there was a booming voice from in front of us.

"Quickly!" the beast growled deeply. "Climb up!"

The dragon was speaking to us!

Then, in the next instant, the creature leaned to the side lowering itself to the ground.

"There is no time for questions!" the dragon continued. "You must trust me! Climb onto my back! It is the only way you'll be safe!"

In the sky above, the dragon that had been attacking us let out an angry wail that I thought was going to curl my hair! Then, the dragon in front of us raised his head to the sky and spat a huge, long tree of fire. The yellow and orange flames lit up everything around us, and for a brief moment, I could see the creature in front of us. He was dark blue, and his skin was rippled and leathery. I wondered if it was the dragon that had dropped the strange black stone in the yard.

"Now!" the dragon screeched. "We must leave now!"

"What is happening?!?!" Kamryn shrieked. "What is that . . . that . . . *thing?!?!*"

"It's a dragon!" I said. "And we'd better do what he tells us!"

I leapt, climbing onto the dragon's back. His skin was warm, thick, and rough. Kamryn was next, and Jason was right behind her.

"Quickly!" the dragon said. "Sit above my wings, near my neck! Hold on tight!"

This was crazy! Twenty minutes ago, I was playing Kick the Can with my friends. Now, I was climbing onto the back of a talking dragon!

But, at least, the dragon seemed to want to help us. I was certain the black dragon attacking us wasn't very friendly . . . and wanted us destroyed.

"Give me the Orb of Shammar!" the dragon ordered.

Huh? I thought. *Orb of Shammar? What was he talking about?*

"The Orb! The Orb!" the dragon exclaimed, his rumbling voice echoing through the yard.

It suddenly occurred to me that he was talking about the black stone in my hand!

I struggled forward and held it out. He reached

back and took it with one claw.

"Now . . . hang on!" the dragon screeched. He stretched his wings, and with a powerful thrust, we were up in the air! The black dragon was behind us, in pursuit, screeching and wailing and huffing fire.

I was holding on around the dragon's neck—as much as I could get my arms around, anyway—and Kamryn had her arms around my waist. Jason was behind her.

As we rose, I could see the lights of Bismarck glowing below us, and could make out the shadows of buildings in the distance. I'd never seen our city from the air before, at night. It looked kind of cool. Houses below—black, rectangular shadows—became smaller as we flew, higher and higher, and streetlights became small, twinkling dots.

And, although the black dragon was still chasing us, we were going faster, pulling away from him quickly. Soon, the only thing behind us was the inky night sky.

We flew in silence for a few minutes. Cool night air rushed past, filling my ears with a loud whooshing noise. Riding on the dragon's back, we flew effortlessly through the darkness.

And I knew right then that I was in a lot of trouble. Mom and Dad would be expecting me home at any minute, and they get really mad if I'm late.

However, being late was going to be the least of my problems. Trouble like I could never have imagined was brewing . . . and Kamryn, Jason, and I were caught right in the middle of it.

12

We flew through the dark, gauzy night, all the while gazing in wonder at the city below. Gradually, my fear faded . . . not completely, though; it was still there, gently gnawing at my belly. I had no idea where we were going, and I was sure that if the dragon made a quick turn or dive, we would be thrown off his back and into the air, falling a long way!

And I don't have to tell you what that would mean!

"Where are we going?!?!" Kamryn shouted from behind me. Over the rushing wind, it was hard to hear her voice.

"Don't ask *me!*" I shouted back. "All I know is that I'm going to wake up in my bed, and this will have been just a bad dream!"

We flew on, higher and higher. The city below vanished, and I could only see speckles of light here and there. Above us, thousands of stars winked. I wondered what Mom and Dad were thinking. No doubt they were looking for me, since I should have been home by now.

But I was more concerned with what was going to happen to us. Sure, the dragon we were riding on didn't seem to want to hurt us. In fact, he had saved us from that other dragon.

And he had spoken! The dragon could actually talk! It was crazy. I felt like I had fallen into a real-life movie or something. Talking, fire-breathing dragons? It just couldn't be real.

Finally, after flying through the darkness for a little while, the dragon turned his enormous head and spoke.

"I think we're far enough away," he said. "He won't find us here."

Suddenly, the dragon turned and dove. It was a quick, unexpected movement, and I held on tight. I could feel Kamryn's arms tighten around my waist as we rapidly descended toward earth. By now, we were some distance from the city, but there were still a few lights below. As we got closer, we could make out a few dark houses here and there, although they weren't as close together as they were on our block. There were a few streetlights glowing, too, and I could make out the dark forms of a few parked cars.

Soon, we were skimming just over the treetops and houses. I have to admit it was kind of cool, and if I hadn't been so freaked out about everything, it would have been kind of fun.

The dragon suddenly turned, and we lowered more, gliding down a street just a few feet from the ground. There was a streetlight up ahead, and the dragon reared back, using his mighty wings to slow. We landed directly beneath the streetlight in a flurry of wings and claws scraping pavement. Finally! We were on the ground, safe. I had no idea what plans the dragon had for us, but at least we weren't flying through the air at a billion miles an hour!

The dragon leaned to the side, and we easily slid off his back. It was a relief to stand on solid ground again, on my own two feet.

But then the dragon turned to face us. I wanted to run, but I knew there was nowhere I could go. I was sure that the dragon could catch me.

And besides, I thought. *The dragon had actually saved us.*

Nevertheless, the three of us stepped back several feet. I wasn't sure if the dragon was going to hurt us, but I didn't want to take any chances, either.

Something else I noticed:

There seemed to be no other people around. There were a few houses with lights on, but we saw no one and heard nothing. Not even any crickets.

The dragon reared back and stretched his neck out. Then, he spread his wings.

And if I'd been freaked out by what had happened so far, it was nothing compared to what was now happening right before our very eyes . . . .

13

The dragon was changing!

At first, I didn't know what was happening. The creature began to shake and shudder and twist and turn, making movements that seemed unnatural. For a moment, I thought he was going to fly off and leave us. Or, maybe he was just going to vanish into thin air.

But that's not what happened. What happened was even *more* amazing.

The beast's form began to change, to move and shift, to wriggle and writhe. He became smaller, too, shrinking to the size of a—

Human! The dragon was taking the shape of a person!

While we watched in amazement, the dragon changed from an enormous, blue beast, into a very human-like form. In a matter of seconds, it was no longer a dragon . . . but a human! And not just a human . . . but a *woman!*

She had very long, silvery hair. In the glow of the streetlight, we could see her bright green eyes. She wore a white robe tied at her waist by what appeared to be a gold rope. In her hands, she held the shiny black stone. She was very pretty, and it was almost impossible to believe that, just seconds before, she had been a fire-breathing dragon.

"You are safe, at least for now," she said, and her voice was very soft. She spoke quietly, calmly, and she sounded nothing at all like she had when she was a dragon. She smiled, and I was relieved. After everything that had happened, I knew now that she meant us no harm.

"Who . . . who are you?" Kamryn asked, in a voice just above a whisper.

"My name is Dori," the woman replied. "I will not hurt you. But you must understand that, although you are safe for the time being, you are still in great danger."

I didn't like the sound of that at all. I already knew I was going to be in trouble for being out later than I was supposed to . . . that was bad enough. Last time I stayed out late without telling Mom or Dad, I was grounded for two weeks. What could be worse than that?

But as Dori began to explain what was happening, I knew she was right: we were in deep trouble . . . trouble that was far, far worse than being grounded for two weeks!

"Perhaps you should sit," Dori said, walking toward us. Her white robe flowed around and behind her as she moved. Her silver hair swayed gently around her head and shoulders, dreamlike.

We did as she suggested, sitting on the curb. Again, I found it very unusual that there was no movement anywhere. No people, nothing. And no sounds.

Very strange.

And for the first time, I got a look at Kamryn and Jason in the light. Kamryn was probably about my age, with shoulder-length blond hair. Jason was a little taller, with short, dark hair. Both were wearing jeans and T-shirts. Jason's shirt was red and had white lettering that read: *Parents for sale! Special! Buy one, get one free!*

Dori walked toward us and stopped. "This will be difficult for you to believe," she began, "but it is true. A war has begun between Dantar, leader of the Night Dragons, and the Keepers of the Emerald Realm. None of these realms are places that humans should be, but now that you are here, in the Emerald Realm, you have only two choices. You can fight or you can flee. If you flee, you will have no place to go. Dantar is a terrible, two-headed beast. His army—the Night Dragons—will most certainly find you. If you join us and fight, your chances of surviving will be better."

"Surviving?" I asked. I didn't like the sound of that.

"The realm you are now in is very different from the one you left behind," Dori said, nodding. "You'll find it is far more dangerous here than it was in your realm."

"Emerald Realm?" Jason said in disbelief as he looked around. "We aren't in any 'Emerald Realm'. It looks like we're on the outskirts of Bismarck, that's all." He glanced around at the few houses up and down the street.

"Yes, I know what it *appears* to look like," Dori continued. "But do you notice anything different?"

"I noticed that there doesn't seem to be anyone around," I replied, "and there aren't any sounds at all, except for us talking."

"That is because for the three of you, time has stopped," Dori replied.

My jaw fell. I looked at Kamryn and Jason. They, too, were baffled.

"But . . . but how can time stop?" Jason asked. "It's not possible."

Dori nodded. "All things are possible," she replied. "You see, the Emerald Realm exists in the spaces between your time. It always has. You, as humans, do not have the ability to see or experience other realms because you are moving through a different space and time. However, you have come in contact with something from our realm. That has brought you to where you are now."

She held up the round, black stone. "By touching this, you have passed into our world. You are now in our realm, caught in the spaces between time. There are thousands of these spaces, and thousands of different realms."

Talk about confusing!

"But that means that time really hasn't stopped," I said. "It just means that we are sort of stuck in a crack."

"Yes, exactly," Dori said with a knowing smile. "All around us, your world is still very much alive . . . however, nothing is moving. Everything is frozen. If you were to look into some of the homes around here, you would see people motionless, not moving."

"What about planes in the sky?" Kamryn asked. "Wouldn't they fall?"

Dori shook her head. "No, because no time is passing. Just because it seems to be passing for you, doesn't mean it's passing at all. It has stopped for you, however, because you are now in our realm."

"But it doesn't look any different than our own world," Jason said again, motioning with his hand.

"Only because you are seeing it with human eyes," Dori said. She smiled. "When you see through dragon eyes, the Emerald Realm will become very clear."

Dori held out the black orb, cradling it in both hands. "Watch," she said.

At first, nothing happened. Soon, however, a faint glow began to appear in the middle of the orb. It began as a pinprick, just a tiny speck of light. While we watched, the light began to grow.

"Is . . . is it like a crystal ball, or something?" Kamryn stammered.

"Watch," Dori repeated.

As we stared in amazement, the glow became brighter. Then the light took on a peculiar shape. Soon, we realized we weren't looking at an orb anymore . . . we were looking at the eye of a dragon . . . and it was looking at us! It was really strange, but kind of cool, too.

While we watched, the black stone began to rise into the air, all by itself. It still looked like an eye, glancing at me, then Kamryn, to Jason, then back to me. It gave me an odd feeling, wondering if, somehow, the mystical orb had a life of its own, if there really was an 'eye' inside, looking back at us, wondering who we were and what we were doing. It was also strange to see the object hovering in the air without any means of support. It just floated in front of us, like a shiny, black softball.

I spoke. "What is—"

But I stopped speaking when I heard what sounded like a rumble of thunder. The sound didn't come from the sky around us, though. Rather, it seemed to be coming from the hovering orb.

That's when we were hit with a bolt of lightning . . . and everything went black.

15

I was aware I was still standing, but everything was completely dark. I blinked my eyes a few times, just to make sure they were open. There had been a blinding flash that seemed to come from all around, and now we were immersed in darkness. I could no longer see lights or homes. Jason, Kamryn, and Dori had vanished.

"What happened?!?!" I heard Kamryn shriek from close by. She sounded completely terrified.

"You're all right," Dori assured us. She was still in front of us, but we couldn't see her. "We've shifted completely into the Emerald Realm. It will take a moment for you to adjust. Be patient, and don't be frightened."

We stood in the darkness, waiting. And when I say 'darkness', I mean it! There was nothing at all to see. Not a speck of light, not a glow . . . nothing. It was eerie, to say the least.

Then, I heard something. Faint at first, but it began to grow louder.

"You should be adjusting," Dori said. "Do you hear or see anything?"

"I hear a creek or a river of some sort," Jason said.

"Yes," Dori replied. "There is a small river not far away. Can you see anything?"

My eyes strained in the darkness. Suddenly, I could see a glow that began to brighten.

"Yeah," I replied. "I can see . . . something."

"Me, too," Kamryn said.

Dori's silhouette began to appear before us. I turned to see the shadows of my two new friends, and a surge of relief rolled through my body. Being in total darkness, without being able to see a single thing, was creepy. Even my bedroom at night, with the lights off, wasn't that dark. There was the constant, comforting glow of the nightlight from the hall, and the faint light and gentle bubbling sounds from our aquarium in the living room.

"Look around," Dori said as the black orb in front of her lowered gently into her hands. It no longer looked like a dragon's eye. "Welcome to my world," she said. "Welcome to the Emerald Realm."

The area around us grew brighter still. As it did, my jaw dropped more and more. Kamryn gasped. Jason drew a deep breath.

What we were seeing was simply unbelievable.

It was a fantasy world.

Gone were the homes around us, the streets, the cars. There were no streetlights, no trees, nothing.

They had been replaced with something else: mountains of ice and rock. At least, that's what it looked like. Sharp, jutting peaks of blue ice and gray rock blended to form jagged, imperfect pyramids. Some looked like they went miles into a reddish-orange sky. Others were only as big as a house. I've seen places like this before, but only in movies and comic books. There was no sun or moon of any sort.

Never in my wildest dreams would I have believed a place such as this could actually exist. Of course, I never thought fire-breathing dragons were real, either!

"Where . . . where is this place?" I asked.

"You haven't gone anywhere," Dori said, knowingly. "The Emerald Realm exists side-by-side, in time, with your world. We have shifted into a different dimension than yours, that's all."

My mind whirled with questions. *How many dragons are there? How many realms? How is all this possible?*

I was quickly overwhelmed when I realized I could no longer think the way I had before. Before, I used reason and common sense to help answer my questions. In my world, there was no such thing as dragons and invisible realms. Now, however, anything and everything seemed possible . . . and probably was.

But if there was any good thing about our situation, it was this: Dori said that time on our 'earthly' realm had stopped for us . . . and that meant I wasn't late getting home. Mom and Dad couldn't be mad at me—yet.

Dori, as if reading my mind, spoke. "I know you have a lot of questions," she said, "and I will answer as many as I can. You must first realize, however, the dangers we are all facing in the Emerald Realm. The Night Dragons are coming, and they will stop at nothing to get what they want."

"What do they want?" Kamryn asked as she pulled a lock of her blond hair away from her face.

"This," Dori replied, holding up the black stone in front of her. "They want the Orb of Shammar, one of the most powerful forces in the universe. With it, there will be no stopping Dantar and his terrible army of Night Dragons. In fact, if they succeed, they'll—"

Dori suddenly stopped speaking and looked into the sky. She turned her head and looked all around.

"What is it?" I asked as I, too, looked up into the sky.

Dori said nothing.

But then, we heard something. It sounded like the low rumble of distant thunder.

"Over there," Kamryn said, pointing into the red-orange sky. "It's a storm cloud. And it's moving fast, too."

"That's no storm cloud," Dori said, shaking her head. Her voice was tense and worried. "That's not a storm cloud at all."

As we watched, I suddenly knew Dori was right. Far in the distance, coming our way, wasn't a cloud . . . it was a living swarm, like hornets.

No, not a swarm—an *army*.

An army . . . of black dragons.

17

"There will be time to explain later!" Dori exclaimed, and her entire body began to twist and turn. In only a few seconds, she had morphed back into a blue dragon, clutching the black orb in a single, leathery claw.

"We must leave! Now!" she exclaimed. Again, her voice surprised me. It was once again deep and gruff. I still found it hard to believe the creature before us was also a human . . . of sorts.

She knelt down, urging us to climb onto her back. I moved first, followed by Kamryn, and then

Jason. In the next moment we were airborne, rising into the sky as the ground fell away.

And what a sight it was! Bismarck, North Dakota, was gone. In every direction, I could see the gigantic ice and stone mountains. Some of them reflected the red-orange sky.

But behind us:

Night Dragons.

They were still a long way off, but we could hear the thundering flurry of their wings as they pounded the air. We could hear their distant screeches, and I could even sense their rage and fury. My skin knotted.

"Where are we going?" I shouted as the wind rushed past. My hair was being blown in a billion different directions.

"Mirage Valley!" Dori replied as we flew faster and faster through the sky.

"Man!" Kamryn shouted from behind me. "If my Mom knew I was doing this, she'd freak!"

"Just think about what you'll be able to tell your friends at school!" Jason yelled from behind her.

I almost laughed. Sure, it would be fun to tell my friends at school that I'd ridden on the back of a dragon and traveled to another realm . . . but who would believe me?

I leaned forward, my arms wrapped tightly around Dori's neck. "What is Mirage Valley?" I asked.

"It is a place where the reflections of the mountains create an illusion," she replied, turning to the left and swooping. "The reflection of the ice and stone are such that it makes it impossible to see what is on the ground. Once we are in the valley, we will be able to see into the sky . . . but the Night Dragons will not be able to see us on the ground. The only thing they will see are mountains of ice and stone."

I turned. Behind us, the seething cloud of Night Dragons was getting closer.

"You'd better hurry!" Jason exclaimed. "They're coming up fast!"

"We're not far," Dori answered. "Don't worry. We'll make it."

But Dori was wrong.

She made a quick turn to the left, and then swooped down, dangerously close to jagged peaks of rock and ice.

"Be careful!" I shouted as we nearly brushed a mountain top.

Dori didn't seem to hear me. We kept flying faster and faster, lower and lower . . . until, all too late, I realized what was about to happen.

Right in front of us was an enormous mountain.

Dori turned . . . but she didn't turn away from it.

She was headed straight for it!

I screamed, and so did Kamryn and Jason. The only thing I could do was close my eyes and wait to slam into the side of the mountain!

18

My arms were a vice-grip around Dori's neck . . . which wasn't going to matter, anyway. After all, we were about to crash into a mountain of rock and ice. And I knew that at the speed we were going, there was no way for Dori to stop in time.

We were doomed, and I knew it.

But after a moment, we hadn't crashed.

I opened my eyes.

We were still high in the air!

How was it possible?!?! Only seconds before, we were on a collision course with a mountain. Now, however, we were still high in the sky. We continued swooping lower, gliding on Dori's powerful wings.

"How . . . how did that happen?!?!" Kamryn hollered from behind me. "I thought we were history!"

Dori turned her head. Her wings were no longer pumping in the air, but held in position as we slowly descended, gliding smoothly. "That's the illusion," she explained. "That's why it's such a good hiding place. From the sky, it only *looked* like we would hit the mountain. But it's only a mirage."

The ground approached as we glided lower and lower. Dori made a few tight turns, then smoothed out. We landed softly, easily.

And just in time, too. Above us, we saw the army of Night Dragons filling the air like a swarm of hideous, deformed bats. They were all black, breathing fire and smoke, and soon, there were so many of them that they darkened the entire sky.

"Are . . . are you sure they can't see us?" I asked Dori. It was odd to talk to a dragon, knowing that he was a she . . . and she was able to turn into human form.

"Yes," she replied, in that deep, husky dragon-voice. "They do not know of Mirage Valley. When they look down, they see mountains of rock and ice, like you saw. The valley makes a good hiding place—especially now, with the Night Dragons searching for us."

"And they're looking for the thing that you have?" Kamryn asked.

Dori nodded, raising her claw to show us the Orb of Shammar. "This is what they want," she replied. "There are perhaps thousands of Dantar's Night Dragons searching for this very stone. If they knew we were here, we would be in a lot of trouble."

I shuddered as the cloud of dragons flew over our heads, high in the sky. We could see them easily, and I hoped Dori was right . . . I hoped they couldn't see us at all.

"But where are the other dragons like you?" Jason asked. "How many are there?"

"Hundreds," Dori replied. "Not nearly as many as there are Night Dragons, however. Now that we are safe—for the time being—I can explain to you what is happening. And I can explain to you what you three must do. You must listen very carefully."

I could tell already that I wasn't going to like what Dori was about to tell us, and as she began to explain, my worst fears were confirmed. It was then that I knew we had to face the fact: Kamryn, Jason, and I might not make it home again.

Ever.

19

Dori changed into her human shape again. It was fascinating to watch. I've seen television shows and movies where things change into entirely different things or objects . . . but that's the work of computer-generated special effects. In real life, watching it happen before our eyes, was really freaky.

"This may take a while to explain," Dori began. She motioned to some large rocks near the edge of an ice and stone wall. "Perhaps we should sit."

"You know," Kamryn said as we walked over to the stones, "with all of this ice, you would think it would be cold."

"That is because the ice here is different than the ice you've experienced," Dori replied. "Remember: you are in another realm. Nothing here can compare to your own world. Here, in the Emerald Realm, our natural laws are completely different."

We sat, and Dori continued. It took her a long time to tell her story. We listened intently, only asking questions when we were confused . . . which was often.

Dori told us that the Orb of Shammar was discovered thousands of years ago in the Emerald Realm. It is very powerful, and is the life-force of all dragons within the realm. She explained it is like the single heart that beats for all in the Emerald Realm. It is the symbol of all that is good in all realms.

"It is so powerful, in fact," Dori said, "that it keeps the terrible Dantar, ruler of the Realm of Darkness and leader of the Night Dragons, a prisoner in his own realm."

However, she explained Dantar knows that if the Orb of Shammar is taken to the Realm of Darkness, it will lose its life-force. Once the Orb of Shammar has been drained of its powers, Dantar will no longer be held prisoner, and he will be able to leave. If that happens, he will use the Sword of Eternal Power to conquer other realms and rule the universe.

"What's the Sword of Eternal Power?" I asked.

"Many thousands of years ago, the Sword of Eternal Power was stolen from the Emerald Realm by invading Night Dragons," Dori explained. "Dantar knew that once he had it, he could use it to begin his conquest of all realms . . . including yours."

Jason spoke. "You . . . you mean—"

Dori nodded her head. "That's right," she replied. "Dantar and his army of Night Dragons are going to take over your world, if they have their way. Thousands of Night Dragons will journey into your realm, through your city."

"Bismarck?!?!" I exclaimed.

Dori nodded. "If that is what you call your city, yes. It is a very special place, and it is the only place in your world where different realms can be entered. If Dantar and his army of Night Dragons invade your world, there will be no stopping them. Human beings, in your realm, would be no match for Dantar's army. And if that happens . . . ."

Dori's voice trailed off. She didn't have to continue. We knew what she meant. If the Night Dragons got their hands on the Orb of Shammar and took it to the Realm of Darkness, the Emerald Realm and all of the dragons within it would no longer exist.

Not only that, our realm—our earthly home—would be in jeopardy.

It was a chilling thought.

But it was nowhere *near* as chilling as what Dori wanted us to do to stop Dantar, and save all of the realms in the universe from destruction.

20

"We must first make sure the Orb of Shammar remains safe," Dori said. "Then, we must capture the Sword of Eternal Power, and use it against Dantar."

"What . . . what do you mean?" Kamryn asked.

"Dantar cannot leave his realm," Dori continued, "because the power of the Orb of Shammar is too great. He lives in a large cave in what is called the Shadow Mountains, in the Realm of Darkness, guarding the sword. But he also flies about the realm, patrolling his domain, waiting and hoping that his Night Dragons will bring him the Orb of Shammar. We must, at all times, keep the orb safe . . . but if we can get the sword, we can use it against him. It will destroy him—and his army of Night Dragons—once and for all."

"You mean steal it?" I asked.

Dori shook her head. "The sword does not belong to him. He cannot use it in a way others can. However, he can use the energy it gives off. Whoever possesses it can wield great power."

"Sort of like a battery?" I asked.

Dori nodded and smiled wide. Her eyes lit up. "Yes!" she exclaimed. "Exactly. Think about this: In your realm you have electricity running through your homes. There are things you use to transfer that electricity to make them work. You have to connect those things to the electricity."

"Yeah," Jason said knowingly. "You plug them into a wall socket. Like a toaster or a vacuum cleaner."

"Yes," Dori said. "This transfers the electricity safely to whatever unit you plug it into. But what would happen if you came in contact with the electricity running through the socket?"

"You'd be electrocuted," Kamryn said with a shudder.

"Exactly," Dori replied. "So, while you're able to safely use the electricity with particular devices, if you came in contact with the electrical current, the results could be terrible."

Now I understood. My dad has always told me that electricity isn't something to be messed with.

"But if the sword is like electricity, who can touch it?" Kamryn asked.

"Someone who is still grounded in their own realm," Dori replied. "Someone who is partially here, but still in their own realm. Someone trapped in time."

I looked at Jason, and he stared at me. Kamryn looked back and forth at both of us, as we realized what Dori was implying.

"You . . . you mean . . . us?" I stammered.

"Yes," Dori said. "Any of you three will be able to use the Sword of Eternal Power without it harming you. You will be able to transfer its energy, much like your 'wall sockets' that you have in your realm."

"But that means we'll have to go to the Realm of Darkness ourselves," I said with growing despair.

Dori nodded. She wasn't smiling. "It won't be easy," she replied. "But it's the only way. I can take you to the Realm of Darkness, but I am powerless to fight Dantar within his own realm. You, on the other hand, are capable of destroying him . . . if you are able to find the Sword of Eternal Power and use it against him. The only thing I know is that it is hidden deep in a cave in the Shadow Mountains. Perhaps even in the very cave where Dantar lives."

I suddenly thought about the situation we were in, and it seemed laughable. Incredible, sure, but laughable. Not long ago, I was hanging out with my friends in Bismarck, North Dakota. Now, I was in another realm, trapped in time, caught in a dragon war.

Bizarre.

"I'd love to help," Jason said, "but we'd better get home. It must be getting late."

Dori shook her head. "Do not forget," she said, "time has stopped. Not a single thing has changed in your realm."

"But can't we just go back to where we were?" I asked. "Can't we just go home?"

Dori shook her head. "It doesn't work that way, I'm afraid," she said. "Remember: I said that our natural laws are very different from yours. While it was easy for you to come to our realm, it will not be easy going back. It will require much power . . . power that can only come from both the Orb of Shammar and the Sword of Eternal Power."

"But that's not fair," Kamryn said. "We don't want to be here."

"You touched the Orb of Shammar," Dori said.

"Whether you want to be here or not, you are here. You are here until Dantar is defeated, or until he is able to get his claws on the Orb of Shammar."

"I didn't touch that thing," Kamryn said. She pointed at me and gave me a nasty look. "He touched me with that rock, and now I'm stuck here."

"And he saved your life by doing so," Dori replied. "If he hadn't, you would have been devoured by the night dragon. I was fortunate enough to find the three of you just in time. Actually, if it is anyone's fault that you're here, it is mine. I dropped the Orb of Shammar by accident, while I was being pursued by one of Dantar's Night Dragons."

Kamryn looked at me sheepishly, apologetic.

"Why did you come to our realm in the first place?" Jason asked Dori.

"The Night Dragons surprised us. Thousands of them invaded our realm, without warning. We knew what they wanted. I hoped that I could slip into your realm with the Orb of Shammar, and hide for a while . . . but one of them spotted me and followed me there."

"Is . . . is he still there?" I asked.

Dori shook her head. "I don't think so," she replied. "He's probably here, in the Emerald Realm. They know that we are here. They know that I have the orb."

"But aren't the Night Dragons attacking your home?" Kamryn asked.

Dori shook her head, and her long, silver hair fell over her shoulders. "They might," she answered, "but they have no interest in destroying our city. All they want is the Orb of Shammar, to take it to Dantar. They will not stop searching until they find it. They will do everything in their power to steal the orb. Here, in Mirage Valley, the Orb of Shammar is safely with me."

Dori spoke too soon.

No sooner had she uttered those words than we heard a flapping of wings. We turned and looked up . . . just in time to see a huge dragon swooping down upon us!

21

Jason, Kamryn, and I leapt up and began to run. Just where we were going, I had no clue . . . but I wasn't going to sit there and let an angry dragon tear us to shreds!

Dori's voice, however, stopped us.

"Wait!" she pleaded. "He's one of us! He's not a Night Dragon!"

We stopped running, skidding to a halt on the hard rock. I turned to see a large, green dragon land in a flurry of huge wings. The beast, standing upright next to Dori's human shape, towered above her.

"Dori!" the creature said urgently as dark smoke drifted from his nostrils. "I hoped I would find you. The Night Dragons know you are here, somewhere in the mountains. If they fly low, they might discover Mirage Valley."

Dori thought about this. She looked worried.

"Then we must hurry," she said. "We must leave Mirage Valley and stop Dantar once and for all."

"But we can't do anything," Jason said. "I mean . . . we're just three kids. We can't fight a giant, two-headed dragon, even with a silly sword."

"It doesn't matter who you are," Dori replied. "It matters if you *believe* you can do it."

"We've got to try," I said. "It's our only way."

Kamryn looked at me, then she looked at Jason. "Damon's right," she said. "Let's do it. It doesn't matter how old we are."

"Okay, what do we do?" Jason said wearily.

"First of all," Dori replied, "you must enter the Realm of Darkness. I can take you there, but I cannot enter myself. There are only a few of us from the Emerald Realm who can survive in such an awful place. I am not one of them."

"But if *you* can't survive," I asked, "how are *we* going to survive?"

Dori smiled and pulled a long lock of her long,

silver hair away from her face. "Remember," she said, "you are still trapped in time. Although you are able to see and experience different realms, you are still secured in your own realm."

We must have looked really confused.

"Please," Dori continued. "I don't have time to explain everything. Just know that if there is anyone who is capable of surviving in the Realm of Darkness, it is you three. You must find the Sword of Eternal Power and use it against Dantar. Let's not waste another moment. I can explain more on our way to the Realm of Darkness."

Suddenly, there was a screech in the sky, and we looked up . . . only to see a huge Night Dragon, as black as coal. He was circling, looking down at us. Then he let out another screech, and a long flame burst from his mouth.

There was no doubt about it: we'd been spotted . . . and this time, our escape was going to be much more difficult—if we were even going to escape at all.

22

In seconds, Dori had changed into a dragon again.

The other dragon spoke. "I'll fight him off while you get away!" he growled, spreading his wings and taking to the air.

"Let's go!" Dori urged us. "Climb up!"

She knelt down and we scrambled onto her back. In seconds, we had taken flight.

Meanwhile, the green dragon was battling with the black dragon. There were bursts of fire and smoke as the two beasts battled in the air, swirling and spinning in a flurry of beating wings. Soon, however, we'd left the two beasts behind as we sailed higher and higher. I looked behind me, thinking that I'd see more Night Dragons attacking. Thankfully, there were none.

But I knew it was only a matter of time. If the Night Dragons wanted the Orb of Shammar as badly as Dori claimed, they'd do everything in their power to get it . . . and take it to Dantar in the Realm of Darkness.

The crazy thing was, that was right where we were headed!

We flew on, over mountains of jagged ice and colorful, rocky plains. We even flew over what appeared to be an ocean, and as I looked in every direction, I could no longer see any land.

All the while, Dori explained what we could expect in the Realm of Darkness.

"It's not really dark," she said. "It's called the 'Realm of Darkness' because there is nothing good there. All things in the realm are terrible and mean. You will encounter things on your journey that you will not understand. There are strange creatures that inhabit the realm, but you must remember that you are stronger than you know. You will be able to survive, but you must think and act quickly."

"But what are *you* going to do?" Kamryn asked, nearly shouting to be heard over the rushing wind.

"I will remain in the Emerald Realm and hide from the Night Dragons, keeping the Orb of Shammar safe while you three search for the Sword of Eternal Power."

Her wings stopped flapping, and we rode an air current, turning to the left. Ahead of us, far below, I could make out an island of some sort. We were coasting on air currents, slowly drifting lower and lower. Ahead of us, the island was getting closer, but now that I could see it better, it didn't look like much of an island at all. In fact, it looked more like a giant, dark whirlpool.

"But what about the sword?" Jason asked. "Where will we find it?"

"Somewhere near Dantar's cave," Dori replied. "It is said that the sword is kept within a glass tomb. The sword's blade gives off a powerful light, so there will be no mistake when you find it. But remember: Dantar will be guarding it, so you must be careful."

We were gliding closer and closer to the surface of the water, heading toward the dark whirlpool. I could see frothy water moving in a circle. In the middle of the whirlpool, the water was moving so fast it created a vertical tunnel, like a huge, black hole that sank into the water.

"What's that?" Kamryn said, pointing to the

swirling water.

"That is the entrance to the Realm of Darkness," Dori replied. "It is here where you must travel through."

By now, we were directly over the whirlpool. The water appeared to be flushing down a giant, dark drain, vanishing into a black hole in the ocean.

"That's the entrance to the Realm of Darkness?!?!" Jason exclaimed. "You mean we—"

"Go to Shadow Mountain!" Dori interrupted. "You will know you are close to Dantar's lair when you reach the petrified forest. Find the Sword of Eternal Power, and destroy Dantar once and for all!"

"Petrified forest?!?!" I shouted "What's—"

All of a sudden, Dori tilted far to the left. I tried to hang on, but there was no way I could do it.

And then, the three of us were tumbling through the air, screaming . . . heading right for the middle of the whirlpool!

23

It was scary enough just falling through the air, but even worse was the fact that we weren't going to land in the water: we were headed straight for the dark eye of the whirlpool created by the churning waters. That was scariest of all, and before we knew it, the water and sky had vanished. I couldn't see Kamryn or Jason, but I could hear them screaming, so I knew they were still close by.

I was terrified. I didn't know where we were headed, but I knew one thing: it was going to hurt. I fell from my bicycle once, and when I hit the grass, I bruised my arm and shoulder. That hurt a lot.

But this was going to be worse. We were pitching through the sky, falling fast, and when we hit something, I knew it was going to be the end of us.

And I couldn't understand why Dori had dropped us the way she did. Since she was from a different realm, maybe she didn't understand that the three of us weren't like her, and we could be hurt easily.

Whatever the reason, I was certain that it was all over for the three of us. Even if we landed in water, we were plummeting so fast it would feel like hitting cement.

Kamryn stopped screaming, and so did Jason. I still couldn't see them.

"Where are you guys?!?!" I shouted. The wind roared in my ears at hurricane force as we continued falling, and I hardly heard my own voice.

"I'm right here!" Kamryn shouted from close by. It was really weird. She sounded like she was only a few feet away, but it was so dark that I couldn't see her!

"Jason!" I yelled. *"Where are you?!?!"*

"Right here!" came his loud reply. I was shocked to hear his voice so close, and I swung my arm out.

"Ow!" he shouted as my arm struck him. *"That*

was my head!"

He grabbed my wrist and held on.

"Kamryn!" I shouted. *"Say something!"*

"I'm here!" she shouted back. *"Right here!"* She sounded like she wasn't too far away, but as I swung my free arm out, I didn't find her. And it was still too dark to see anything.

All the while, I waited for the inevitable. I knew we would suddenly slam into something, without warning, and that would be the end of us. After all, we were falling very, very fast. When we hit the ground or anything, we'd probably break every bone in our bodies.

Suddenly, something grabbed my ankle.

"Kamryn!" I shouted. "Is that you?!?!"

"Yes!" she screamed. "Grab my hand!"

"I can't see it!" I replied.

"I'm reaching up!" she said. "Reach down and grab my hand!"

I reached down and flailed my hand about. After a moment, I felt the smooth skin of her arm.

"Gotcha!" I said, and I pulled.

Now, the three of us were together, holding hands. We were together, but we were still falling, faster and faster, plummeting toward—

Toward what?

Then, I noticed that we weren't wet. Although we'd fallen right through the dark middle of the whirlpool, no water had touched us at all!

"Hey, look!" Jason shouted.

"What?!?!" I shouted back.

"Below us!" he exclaimed. "It's getting brighter!"

It was!

Beneath us, the darkness was giving way to a murky gray. There wasn't anything to see, but it appeared that it was getting lighter.

Another scary thing: we couldn't tell which way was up or down. Or, if there even *was* an up or down. It was a terrifying feeling: not only to be falling, but not able to see a single thing.

And then—we could see something.

Beneath us.

"What's that?!?!" Kamryn shrieked.

But we didn't have to answer. We all knew what it was; we all knew what was about to happen.

Beneath us, the ground had appeared . . . and we were only seconds from hitting it at a bajillion miles an hour!

24

We started screaming again, since we knew that when we hit the ground, it was going to be the end of us. There was nothing we could do.

The ground rushed toward us, faster, faster, until finally, I closed my eyes. I was still screaming my head off, but I closed my eyes and prepared myself for the worst.

And then—

We hit.

But what we hit was totally unexpected. It was like we'd landed in some sort of gigantic sponge! The ground wasn't hard at all. In fact, it was very soft, like a huge feather pillow. Instead of hitting a hard-packed surface, our fall was broken by a soft cushion. In fact, it didn't hurt a single bit.

The soft, buoyant ground gently accepted our weight. Then it bounced back, and we tumbled about. The feeling was like being on a giant bed, all gentle and smooth.

"Okay," Kamryn said as she lay on her back, staring up into the sky. "That's it. Wake me up, because this has got to be a nightmare."

"If it is, I'm having it, too," Jason said, rolling to his side.

"Me, too," I echoed, propping myself up on my elbows and looking around. "Where are we?"

"It's the Realm of Darkness that Dori told us about," Kamryn said. "And it's not dark at all, just like she said."

And it wasn't. The sky was dark gray . . . all except for directly above us. There was a gaping black hole, and I knew it was the strange funnel that we'd fallen through. Around us, there was nothing else to see at all. No mountains, no trees. The only thing we could see was where the sky met the earth, far, far away. There was nothing for miles and miles.

"Are we going to have to go back through there

to get out of here?" Jason asked.

"I don't know," I replied. "But you heard what Dori said: we've got to find that sword and use it against that two-headed dragon."

"But there's nothing here," Kamryn said. "Look around. There's nothing to see at all. There isn't even a path or a road to follow. It's like we landed on a gigantic gray marshmallow."

"I wish I'd never gone outside," Jason said. "If I hadn't, I wouldn't be here."

"And I wish I'd never tried to scare you," Kamryn said. "I'd be watching television at this very moment, and getting ready for bed."

"I'm not going to wish for anything but a way out of here," I said. "I wish that we find that sword, and fast."

Oh, I'd get my wish, that was for sure. But soon, I'd be wishing for something else . . . I'd be wishing that we'd escape with our lives.

Trouble was, I didn't know if it was a wish that would be granted . . . and that scared me a lot.

25

Jason struggled and stood up. "Well, we'd better head somewhere," he said. "Staying here is going to get us nowhere fast."

But here was the problem: the ground was so soft that we sank up to our knees in the foamy cushion. There was no support at all, and walking was going to be nearly impossible. We'd have to crawl on our hands and knees, like we were in some vast moonwalk. I tried to walk, but my foot just sank into the soft earth.

"This isn't going to work," I said in frustration.

"We can't walk on this stuff."

But there was something else we *could* do.

Kamryn made a quick, bouncing motion, and found that the soft cushion beneath us acted like rubber. Just an easy movement propelled her a couple of feet into the air. She landed on one foot and bounced forward, landed on her other foot and continued, making huge leaps of twenty feet or more!

I tried to do the same, and quickly got the hang of it. Soon the three of us were running—bouncing, in fact—taking fantastic leaps.

"Wow!" Jason shouted as he bounced into the air. "I'd be able to jump over a car if there was one around!"

"The good news is that we can cover a lot of ground easily," I said as I made another leap. It was kind of cool.

But I was constantly reminded of the terror I had felt as we'd fallen down the dark eye of the whirlpool, and I knew our strange adventure was far from over. After all: Dori had warned us that we would come across strange creatures.

We bounced and bounced, taking giant strides and making large leaps. After a short while, Jason slowed, and, instead of bouncing forward, he leapt up into the sky, as high as he could go. He must have gone fifty feet into the air!

"There's something over there!" he said, pointing as he came back down. He hit the soft cushion, only to bounce high into the air again. "Over there! I see something! It looks like a mountain or something!"

Kamryn and I did what Jason did, bouncing straight up into the air. The feeling was a lot like being on a trampoline . . . only we could bounce a lot higher!

And Jason was right. Far in the distance, we could see what appeared to be a single mountain, rising up from the ground. It was a long way away, but there was no doubt that the mountain was big . . . probably bigger than anything we had in our earthly realm. I was certain it was Shadow Mountain.

Where Dantar, the terrible two-headed dragon lived.

"That's got to be fifty miles from where we are!" Kamryn said as she bounced high and looked into the distance.

"Yeah, but we've probably already gone fifty miles," I said. "It shouldn't take us long to get there. Let's keep going."

"What was that Dori said about the petrified forest?" Kamryn asked.

"She said something about Dantar living near

there," I replied.

"What's 'petrified' mean?" Jason asked.

"It means 'frozen' or hard," I replied, very matter-of-factly.

"How do *you* know?" Jason challenged, as if I was making up the definition.

"Because I read books," I said. "And when I find a word I don't know, I look it up in the dictionary. In fact, if—"

It was at that instant we heard a terrible wail. It was far away, and high in the sky, but the three of us could hear it clearly.

We turned to look . . . and my blood ran cold. What we saw was horrifying beyond belief.

26

In the sky, far away, was the two-headed dragon.

Dantar.

His wings appeared to flap slowly, dreamlike, as if burdened by his sheer size and weight. He was a dark, bluish-purple, and had a long tail. One head was lowered, moving from side to side. The other head was cocked up, and while we watched, it blew a huge blast of fire.

Fortunately for us, the beast wasn't headed toward us. Which was a good thing, because I don't think there would be any way we would have been able to outrun it. I don't know how fast dragons can travel, but I was sure that a creature that big, with huge, powerful wings, could travel very fast . . . even faster than we could bounce, which was pretty fast.

And another thing we realized: the dragon was headed toward the mountain. Oh, from where we stood, we couldn't be sure, but it looked like he was headed in the direction in which we'd spotted the super-huge rock formation.

"I'm not picking a fight with that thing!" Jason said defiantly. By now, the two-headed dragon was nearly out of sight.

"We have to," I said. "Besides . . . remember what Dori told us? We don't have any other choice."

"Except to find that sword and get rid of that giant, fire-burping purple iguana," Kamryn said.

"Right," I agreed with a nod. "Let's wait a couple of minutes, until we can't see the dragon at all. Then, we'll keep heading for Shadow Mountain."

And that's what we did. When Dantar was gone, we began bouncing our way toward the mountain. Soon, we could see it without bouncing high into the air. A while later, it loomed high above us, and I realized that my earlier thoughts were right: the mountain was bigger than anything we had on earth, in our own realm. Shadow Mountain seemed to go up into the sky forever.

"So that's where he lives," I said. "Somewhere inside."

"We've just got to find out where," Kamryn said.

"Yeah," Jason added. "Before he finds us."

Problem was, at the time, we didn't have to worry about Dantar finding us. Dori had warned us there were other creatures to worry about . . . and at that very moment, one of them was about to attack.

27

Here's what happened:

Now that we were closer to the mountain, we could see it was made up of solid rock, but we couldn't be sure. After all, it could be made up of the same stuff that we had been bouncing on. There were no trees anywhere, and the atmosphere was cold and lifeless. The sky above remained cold, iron-gray, impersonal, and ominous.

As we approached the mountain, we could see smaller mountains, like foothills. Although the foothills were nowhere near the size of Shadow Mountain, they were still pretty big.

What we didn't see right away were the small caves nearly hidden all around and up and down the foothills.

"Now what?" Jason asked as we stopped bouncing. As we stood in the soft, cushion-like earth, we looked up at the looming mountain, and at the foothills not far away.

"Well, we saw that giant dragon head this way," I said. "He's got to be around here somewhere."

"Let's not worry about finding Dantar," Kamryn said, "until we find that sword Dori told us about."

"Let's keep moving," I said. "There's nothing around here."

It was easier to hop than walk, but as we got closer to the foothills, the ground beneath our feet became harder and more solid, more like the ground in our own realm. We bounced less and less, and soon, we had slowed to a steady walk.

"Wait," Kamryn said as she stopped walking. She had a puzzled look on her face as she pointed toward the foothills. "What's that?"

At first, I couldn't see anything. The foothills were a light, sandy-brown color. As a matter of fact, there wasn't much color to be seen anywhere. The sky was gray, the ground we were walking on was gray, and the mountains were a dull brown. I would hate to have to live here. There were no bright colors, anywhere. Everything looked boring and cheerless.

"What do you see?" Jason asked.

"I'm not sure," Kamryn said. "But I thought I saw something move over there. It looks like there's some sort of cave over there, part way up that hill."

I looked, but I didn't see anything . . . at first. Then, I *did* see something move. I couldn't tell what it was, but Kamryn and Jason saw movement, too.

And Kamryn was right: there was some sort of cave in the side of the hill. As I glanced around, I saw several more scattered about, at various levels on the foothills. But the reason that it was difficult to see them was because each cave had what appeared to be a large boulder blocking its entrance.

We waited for a moment, thinking we might see something move, but nothing did. Everything was still and quiet.

Too still and quiet.

"I guess I was just imagining things," Kamryn said. She began to walk, and Jason did, too.

But not me. I was glancing around, looking around the foothills . . . when I saw more movement.

"Wait," I said, pointing. "You were right, Kamryn. Something moved up there."

Kamryn and Jason stopped walking. We stood, staring at the desolate foothills and the monstrous mountain that loomed up behind them.

Suddenly, one of the boulders moved. It began to rise up, and it was then I realized it wasn't a boulder at all . . . it was the head of a hideous, snake-like monster!

Before we knew what was going on, other beasts were emerging, wiggling out, rising up on their thick, stalk-like bodies. There were over a dozen of them. They were brown, just like their surroundings, and they blended in perfectly . . . which was why we had such a hard time seeing them. Their bodies appeared to have scales like a snake, but I couldn't be sure because they were too far away. They wriggled and squirmed as they rose from their caves, like monstrous caterpillars without legs.

And without any warning at all, the giant, snake-like creatures lunged forward and attacked!

28

The three of us turned and ran in the opposite direction. Fortunately for us, the ground became soft again. The more our feet sank, the bigger the jumps we could take. We kept bouncing until I looked back over my shoulder to see the strange beasts writhing like snakes. Lucky for us, they could only go so far, like they were somehow tethered to their holes.

Maybe that's what they are, I thought. *Giant snakes. After all . . . Dori had told us to watch out for strange creatures.*

"I think we can stop now," I huffed. I was

breathing hard, and I gulped down air to catch my breath.

Jason and Kamryn took another long bounce, then stopped. They, too, were out of breath.

"We're going to have to be more careful," Kamryn said. "Those things could have eaten us alive!"

"It's kind of hard when we don't know what to look for," Jason said.

"We're looking for the sword and the dragon," I replied. "But Kamryn's right: we have to really be careful."

In the distance, the long, snake-like creatures were pulling back. We watched them as they retreated to their holes and became nearly invisible, with just their heads poking out from their caves. It was easy to miss them, because they were camouflaged very well.

"Let's make our way around the mountain and see what's there," I said, "only we'll keep our distance. There might be other creatures hiding in the foothills."

"I should have brought my camera," Jason said. "Nobody at home is going to believe this."

"But maybe we could write a book," I said.

Kamryn's eyes grew huge. "We'll be famous!" Kamryn exclaimed.

"We'll be rich!" Jason chimed. "We'll probably even get our own book deal and make millions!"

"First, let's just concentrate on getting home alive," I said.

We bounced off, making giant leaps and covering great distances. All the while, my eyes scanned the foothills, searching for any more of those long, wiry beasts—or any other creature, for that matter. Dori had told us to be on the lookout for anything.

But it never occurred to me to look up into the sky. I was too busy searching the base of the mountain and the foothills.

So, when I heard an awful snarl and a loud, angry screech, I threw my head back, looked up . . . and screamed.

29

In the split second between the time I heard the noise and the time I looked up, I thought I was going to see a Night Dragon, or worse: the enormous, two-headed form of Dantar.

It was neither.

What it was, I couldn't tell. The creature was the size of a car. It looked like it could have been a bird, but it had fur instead of feathers. It was a dusty gray color, and had a curved, black beak, like a hawk. Maybe that's what it was—some sort of weird, furry bird of prey.

The problem was this: we were going to be the prey!

The bird came straight down at us. Its legs were extended, reaching out to snare us with its claws. Kamryn and Jason also saw the huge bird-creature swooping down, and the three of us took gigantic leaps in opposite directions—and that's what saved us.

But not for long.

By springing up from the cushiony ground, we were able to leap dozens of yards away from the bird. We were lucky, because if we would have been on normal ground, we probably wouldn't have been able to escape.

The menacing bird, however, wasn't going to go away. He wouldn't be able to get all three of us, but he could certainly get one of us . . . and that someone was going to be Kamryn.

At first, the bird turned and started after me. Then, it spun quickly and headed in Kamryn's direction. She made a strong, long bounce that sent her high into the air . . . and that was her mistake. The bird was very fast, and was able to catch up with her before she landed and could make another leap.

"Kamryn!" I shrieked.

"No! No!" Jason cried, horrified.

It was too late. The awful bird snared Kamryn

from the sky with its long talons. We could see Kamryn struggle, but we couldn't do anything but watch as the bird-creature turned with its mighty wings, and carried Kamryn away.

30

"We've got to do something!" Jason screamed. "That big, ugly flying thing just stole my cousin! She owes me five bucks from last week!"

"Let's go after it!" I shouted. "It's flying low enough for us to reach her, if we can catch up to the thing!"

Just what we would do if we *did* catch up to it I wasn't sure. But we had to do *something*.

We didn't waste another precious second. Jason and I sprang, bounding into the air, taking giant leaps, trying to catch up with the fleeing furry-bird-creature that still held Kamryn in its clutches.

"We're getting closer!" I shouted as we continued bounding across the soft earth. However, the strange bird was headed toward the mountain and the foothills, where the ground was harder. If we didn't catch up with Kamryn and the creature soon, we wouldn't be able to jump as high or move as fast.

Plus, we had another problem: what would we do if we were able to reach the creature? The thing was a lot bigger than we were. With its sharp beak and talons, it would probably tear us to shreds.

Either way, we were going to find out, as it only took a few more bounces, and we were beneath the bird-creature. I could see Kamryn held tightly within the beast's grasp. She was pounding on its legs with her fists and screaming.

"Put me down!" she was saying, over and over. *"You're ugly and this is not funny! Put me down!"* It was actually sort of funny, in a horrifying sort of way. She must have been really frightened, but she still had it within her to try to fight off the winged beast, demanding that it let her go.

"What now?!?!" Jason shouted.

"Jump up and try to grab her!" I said. "Maybe the thing isn't strong enough to carry all three of us!"

I mustered all my strength, and leapt. Jason did,

too. The soft, springy cushion beneath our feet sent us high into the sky, up, up, closer, closer still—

"Kamryn!" I shouted. She hadn't been watching, but my shout from close by attracted her attention, and she turned . . . just in time to reach out her hand and grab mine. I felt something tighten around my ankle, and I looked down to see Jason holding on. The ground below rolled by like a conveyor belt.

"This thing won't let me go!" Kamryn was yelling. Her blond hair was tangling in the wind, washing all over her face.

"Don't let go!" I shouted up to her. Then, I looked down at Jason, gripping my ankle with both hands. "Don't you let go, either!" I shouted to him.

Very quickly, it became obvious my plan wasn't going to work. The flying beast showed no signs of weakening. In fact, it was carrying us higher into the sky, over the foothills.

Which posed another problem.

Suppose it drops us, right now, I thought. *When we were walking near the foothills, the ground was hard. If this thing drops us now, or if we fall, we'll hit solid ground!*

But that wasn't our biggest problem. Our biggest problem was those long, snake-like monsters that were no longer hiding in their holes . . . because they'd spotted us. They'd spotted us, and were now rising into the sky, reaching up, attacking like mad cobras!

31

Jason screamed as one of the creatures came at him like a bolt of lightning, missing him by only a few inches. Another one reared up, snaking high into the sky, but he wasn't long enough to reach us.

It was weird: a minute ago, I was hoping the bizarre, winged creature would lower us to the ground. Now I was hoping he'd fly higher, so we wouldn't get eaten by the long, rope-like monsters!

Thankfully, that's what the bird did. It rose higher, out of reach of the strange snakes. It was a relief. Not much, but a little relief, at least.

The foothills were soon far beneath us, and Shadow Mountain loomed off to our right. And I couldn't be sure, but it looked like that's where we were heading: closer and closer to the mountain.

Jason was still holding onto my ankle with both hands. "Pull yourself up!" I shouted down to him.

"I'm trying, but I can't!" he yelled back up.

"You're too heavy!" I shouted back. "I can't hold on much longer!"

"Hey!" Kamryn hollered. "It's *me* who's doing all the work! I'm holding onto *both* of you, and I'm not going to be able to for very long!"

As fate would have it, we wouldn't have to hold on much longer. As we approached the mountain, the strange bird-like creature swooped lower. Beneath us, trees came into view. Or, what *looked* like trees . . . at first. As we got closer, I could see they appeared to be made of solid rock! There were no leaves, just limbs, and as we came closer still, I could see hundreds of them. They looked exactly like tall, dead trees, except for the fact that they were made of rock.

In one tree, however, we saw a dark spot. It looked like some sort of nest . . . and there was something moving in it!

"What's that?!?!" Jason shouted from beneath me.

"It looks like a nest of some sort!" I called back.

"Yeah, and that's where this thing is taking us!" Kamryn shouted.

Kamryn was right. The giant bird made a quick, low swoop, and Jason yelped as he almost lost his grip. The wind whipped at my hair. We could now see what appeared to be a nest made of stone. Sitting down in it were three baby creatures. They looked like baby birds, covered with gray fuzz. Their wings were tiny and undeveloped. But, even as babies, they were bigger than we were!

All too late, we realized what was about to happen. As we drew near, the baby creatures craned back their necks and opened their beaks. They shifted and jockeyed about, and began making weird, gulping noises.

Oh, no! We were going to be bird food!

32

I didn't know what to do. If I let go, or if Kamryn let go, the three of us would fall to the ground, where we'd wind up flat as pancakes.

But being gobbled up by three hungry bird creatures didn't sound like a lot of fun, either!

Then, before I had a chance to make a decision, the bird-creature dropped us . . . right into the nest, next to the giant baby birds. I tumbled onto Jason, and Kamryn fell on top of us. The short fall knocked the wind out of us, but we weren't hurt . . . yet.

But we were now face to beak with three huge

baby bird-creatures!

We quickly scrambled apart and crawled away, backing up against the side of the nest. All the while, the three humongous baby creatures glared at us with enormous beady eyes. They looked puzzled, like they weren't sure of what we were or whether they should eat us or not. They were no longer making weird noises, and their beaks were closed, but that didn't mean they weren't dangerous.

And, thankfully, the mother creature had flown off, perhaps in search of more food.

Jason, Kamryn, and I just stood there, frozen to the nest, gasping for breath, watching the three weird creatures glare at us. They were actually taller than we were, and they had huge, glossy eyes that blinked every few seconds.

"I . . . I think they're afraid of us," Kamryn whispered.

"I think you're right," I whispered back. *"We probably don't look like the food their mother normally brings them."*

I turned and looked down, outside the nest. We were high in the air, but there were a lot of stone branches, so we might be able to climb down.

Suddenly, I realized something.

"Jason! Kamryn!" I exclaimed. "This is the

petrified forest that Dori told us about! She said that Dantar's home was near the petrified forest! That's where we are!"

Jason and Kamryn snapped around and looked down.

"Then, let's get out of here before these three things change their minds about their meal!" Kamryn said.

"Or, before their mother comes back!" Jason said.

The nest was made of stones, assembled like bricks in the crook of the petrified tree. I was first to climb up and over the side, lowering myself to a nearby branch. I glanced down to see the ground, far below. If I fell now . . . .

Don't even think about it, Damon, I ordered myself. *You're a good tree climber. This isn't any different. You can do this.*

At least, that's what I *told* myself.

"Be careful," Kamryn said.

As soon as I was on the branch and nestled close to the trunk of the tree, Kamryn began to climb down. Jason followed, and the three of us carefully scrambled down, holding onto to stone limbs and hoping we wouldn't fall . . . and hoping that the mother bird wouldn't come back. It was difficult. On one hand, I wanted to get down as fast as I could . . . but I knew that if I wasn't careful, I might lose my grip and fall. Then, it would be all over.

Then again, if that mother bird—or whatever she was—came back, that wouldn't be good, either.

Thankfully, we made it to the ground safely, and we didn't see any more of the flying creature. And there didn't appear to be any of those long, snake-like things hiding in any caves.

"Now which way?" Kamryn asked as she searched the sky.

I looked around, then pointed to the mountain that loomed before us. "Might as well go that way," I said.

We started out. Here, the ground beneath our feet was solid, so it was easy going. It was a lot different than the soft, sponge-like ground we'd been able to bounce across a little while ago.

While we walked, we talked about what we'd experienced so far.

"Nobody is going to believe us, ever," Jason said.

"No way," Kamryn agreed, shaking her head. "In fact, I'm not sure *I* believe it . . . and it's happening to me right now!"

"That doesn't make any sense," Jason said.

"None of this makes sense," I said. "That's the point. This whole idea of different worlds in different realms is crazy."

"But those dragons were real," Kamryn said.

I nodded as I stepped over a rock. "And that thing that carried us to the nest was, too. And the two-headed dragon we saw was real. It's real, all right."

"Yeah," Kamryn said. "It's *real* crazy."

Suddenly, Jason stopped walking. "Hold on a second, guys," he said.

I stopped, and so did Kamryn.

"What's wrong?" Kamryn asked.

Jason was staring down, looking at his feet. "Don't you feel it?" he asked.

The three of us stood for a moment, staring down at the ground, not speaking. I didn't know what Jason was talking about . . . at first. And then, I *did* feel something.

The ground beneath our feet was trembling, harder and harder with every passing second!

"What is it?!?!" Kamryn shrieked. Her head snapped around as she frantically looked at the ground around her.

"I think it's an earthquake!" Jason shouted.

That freaked me out. I'd never been in an earthquake before, and I didn't know what to do. Were we supposed to run? If so, where? What if the ground opened up and we fell into a deep hole or something? I was terrified.

But it wasn't anything compared to the terror I felt when I looked behind us . . . and realized that the trembling earth wasn't caused by an earthquake . . . it was caused by the giant steps of something far, far worse.

Dantar.

The terrible, two-headed dragon.

And there was no mistake about it: he had spotted us.

He had spotted us . . . and he didn't look like he was dropping in to say 'hello'!

33

Dantar looked absolutely *hideous*. It was a word I'd learned in school last year, and it was the only word I could use to describe the two-headed beast that was quickly bearing down on us. He was walking on two huge legs. Smoke steamed from the creature's nostrils, and, while we watched in horror, the left head sent a long, blazing plume of fire up into the sky. His wings were spread, as if he were ready to take flight at any moment.

But his eyes . . . both sets of them . . . were upon us. We knew that he was after us, and if we didn't do something quickly, we'd never get away.

Of course, our chances weren't looking all that good at the moment, but we couldn't just stand there!

So, we did the only thing we could do: we ran. We were still at the bottom of the huge mountain, and there were lots of giant, petrified trees all around. We darted among them as the ground beneath our feet trembled with every step the two-headed dragon took.

And he was getting closer, but we still hadn't spotted anywhere to hide. The ground shook with every step he took, and we was powerful enough to knock over stone trees, sending debris crashing to the ground.

I glanced at some of the enormous stone tree trunks as we ran passed them . . . and that gave me an idea. The tree trunks were big—three or four times our size. Maybe we could hide behind them! Maybe Dantar would pass us by, not knowing we were hiding behind the trunks!

It was worth a shot.

"There's only one thing we can do!" I shouted as I ran. "We've got to hide among the trees! Pick a tree and hide behind it! Maybe Dantar won't see us!"

"You're crazy!" Jason said.

"Maybe!" I yelled back. "But it's our only chance! We'll never outrun him!" I managed a quick glance behind me. The forest had become thicker, but I could still make out the giant, two-headed dragon coming after us. He was easily as big as a four-story building, and as he made his way through the petrified trees, their branches made awful crunching sounds as the dragon knocked them down.

"Damon's right!" Kamryn said. "Maybe we can hide! Maybe he'll pass right by us!"

I picked a tree, ran to the other side of the stone trunk, and fell back against it. The ground beneath me trembled even more. I watched Jason as he, too, chose a large trunk and hid behind it. A few feet from me, Kamryn had found a tree trunk and stopped, too.

"Hey!" she gasped. "This one has a split in it! I can hide inside!" She wriggled and squirmed and soon, she vanished. Kamryn, for sure, would be hidden, but Jason and I were out in the open. Our only hope was that the terrible two-headed beast didn't see us.

The ground shook even more . . . so much so that I thought I was going to fall down. I tried to hold onto the tree trunk, but that didn't help very much.

Stone branches began to fall all around me, and I realized too late that my plan had one fatal flaw: if one of those heavy, petrified branches landed on me, I'd be squished like a bug. In fact, right then, a branch crashed down right in front of me! And that meant—

I managed a glance up . . . only to see two heads swaying back and forth, searching, scouring the ground. As Dantar continued moving forward, I slowly inched my way around the tree. Stone branches crashed down all around me. All I could do was remain pressed against the trunk and hope the beast didn't see me.

Finally, the dragon had passed by, leaving a jumbled mess of broken stone branches. I hadn't been spotted! I glanced over at Jason, and he, too, had done the same thing, flattening himself against the petrified tree trunk, hoping he would remain out of sight of Dantar. The trembling beneath our feet began to fade as we watched the two-headed dragon continued to plow a path through the petrified forest, searching for us.

When I thought it was safe, I darted from my hiding place and ran to Jason.

"That was close!" he gasped.

"Too close," I agreed.

We sprang to the tree where Kamryn was hiding. Sure enough, there was a split at the base of the trunk, just big enough to wiggle through.

"Kamryn," I called. "It's okay. You can come out now."

There was no answer.

I leaned closer. "Kamryn?" I poked my head through the split in the trunk.

Kamryn was gone! What's worse, there was a large, dark hole on the inside of the tree, leading down! A cool breeze from the hole whispered at my cheeks.

"Kamryn!" I shouted into the trunk, and I could hear my voice echo and echo and echo . . . until it finally faded away.

My heart sank as I realized what had happened. Not knowing there was a hole there, Kamryn had crawled into the tree trunk to hide . . . only to fall, vanishing into the depths of the earth. She had probably screamed, but with the noise of the approaching dragon, we hadn't heard her.

"What's the matter?!?!" Jason asked. His voice trembled with fear and panic.

I pulled back . . . and gave him the bad news.

"Your cousin is gone," I said. I pointed to the base of the stone tree. "Kamryn fell down a deep hole. I don't think she saw it when she crawled into the tree trunk."

His eyes widened and his hands flew up, covering his mouth to stifle a gasp of horror. Tears welled up in his eyes. "She owed me five bucks, too," he said remorsefully. He sniffed. "That's a lot of money."

There was no doubt about it.
Kamryn was gone.

34

We stood at a ridge of the mountain, staring down. Jason and I had been climbing for what seemed like days. We were tired, and we were sad. Jason had lost his cousin, (and his five bucks) and I'd lost a new friend. I really liked Kamryn . . . but now I knew that I wouldn't see her again.

And I was angry, too. Now, more than ever, I wanted to defeat the two-headed dragon. Not only to keep the Night Dragons from invading our world, but I wanted to avenge Kamryn, too. We had to do it for her. After all, it hadn't been her fault she'd been dragged into this mess . . . it had been mine. I was the one who had brought her into this strange realm.

But our whole ordeal had really become overwhelming. We weren't exactly sure where to find the sword that Dori had spoken of. All we knew was that it would be close to Dantar's lair. And even if we *did* find it, that didn't mean we'd know how to use it . . . or that we'd be able to find Dantar. Our only hope was to find the sword, and then let the dragon find us.

We weren't at the top of the mountain, but we were close. Beneath us, a ridge separated a deep valley filled with huge, jutting peaks and towering petrified trees.

"What's that?" Jason asked, pointing into the valley before us.

At first, I didn't see what he was pointing at. Then I spotted it: a large, dark cave carved into the rock wall at the bottom of the canyon.

What's more, there appeared to be thin tendrils of smoke drifting out of it, rising up into the air.

"I'll bet that's where he lives," I said with a shudder. "I'll bet he's in there right now, snoozing."

Jason nodded and looked at me. "But where's the sword?" he wondered aloud. "Dori said it would be close by. Do you think he has the sword with him, inside the cave?"

"Maybe," I said. "But there's only one way to know for sure."

Jason looked at me, but he didn't say anything. He knew what I meant. Oh, he didn't like the idea at all, but he knew what we had to do.

We had to hike down into the valley and enter the cave. As crazy as it sounded, that's what we would have to do.

I watched as a puff of smoke drifted out from the distant cave, twirled, rose up, and disappeared.

"Well, then," Jason said, placing his hands on his hips. "Let's get this over with."

He started out and I followed, stepping around large rocks and jutting slabs of stone as we made our way deep into the valley . . . toward the lair of Dantar, the terrible two-headed dragon.

35

Climbing down into the valley proved to be easier than I thought it would be. There were a lot of rocks we had to go around, and we had to be careful to watch for ledges and peaks that jutted out, because we certainly didn't want to fall. Luckily the ground wasn't all that steep, and we didn't have any trouble making it to the bottom of the valley. And we weren't surprised by any more weird creatures.

All the while, I kept glancing in the direction of the dark cave in the distance, looking for signs of Dantar. We could still see whiffs of smoke curling out and up, and I wondered if the beast was sleeping. I hoped he was, and I hoped he wouldn't wake up soon. The last thing we needed was for him to wake up and see us.

But if we could surprise him, if we could somehow find the sword—even if it was in the cave with him—we might have a chance.

But what do we do with the sword once we find it? I wondered. Dantar was gigantic. Surely, a little sword wouldn't do much to stop the huge creature.

Then again, Dori had said that the sword was very powerful. In just what way, I didn't know . . . but I had to trust her. We didn't have any other choice.

"Let's get closer," I said quietly, and we started out across the valley. The cave was still a long way away, but, oddly enough, I didn't feel tired. We'd bounced across the strange, spongy plain; climbed a mountain, and descended into a valley . . . but I still felt strong and alert. Normally, I would have been exhausted, but I felt fine.

As we drew closer to the cave, we were careful to try to stay hidden behind large boulders. In case the dragon appeared, we wanted to remain out of sight.

Looming ahead of us, the cave was nothing but a wall of inky blackness, with thick strands of smoke puffing out. There was no visible sign of Dantar, but

Jason and I were certain we'd found his home.

When we were about a hundred feet away, we stopped behind a large rock, peering around it. Ahead of us, the dark cave rose up. Thin wisps of smoke were still seeping from the top of the cave. We heard no sounds at all—no wind, nothing.

"I'll bet he's in there," Jason whispered.

"I'll bet you're right," I agreed. *"But what do we do? Where's the sword?"*

"What if we have to go inside the cave to get it?" Jason asked.

"I'm not going in there," I said quietly. *"Not while that two-headed, overgrown lizard is in there."*

"Maybe he's sleeping," Jason said. *"Maybe we could wait until he wakes up. When he leaves, we can go inside and look for the sword."*

We wouldn't have long to wait. Not two seconds after Jason spoke, we heard a deep, throaty rumble from the cave. It was loud enough to shake the earth beneath our feet. A dark, thick puff of smoke came from the cave.

Then—silence.

"Maybe one of his heads burped," Jason whispered, and I almost laughed out loud. There was something funny about a two-headed dragon burping.

We didn't dare move. The two of us remained

motionless, staring into the dark cave searching for—

Suddenly, we saw movement. A chill shot down my spine, and I hoped I was out of sight.

Then, in the shadows of the cave, I made out two snouts, each dripping black smoke. And two pairs of red, glowing eyes. Although I still couldn't see the creature, I could tell just by the size of the noses that the beast was gigantic.

And before we knew what was happening, fire erupted from the creature's two mouths, and hot, yellow flames flowered all around us!

36

My first thought was to run, but I knew that we couldn't. Fortunately, being behind the large rock saved us. The flames twirled all around, but the rock blocked them from reaching us.

But it was *hot!* Jason and I dropped to our knees and curled up on the ground, trying to stay away from the boiling yellow fire that swirled all around.

Seconds later, the flames were gone, and the air cooled. I frantically checked my clothes to make sure I wasn't on fire.

Finding nothing, I rolled over and peered

around the rock. Dantar was emerging from his cave, his two heads writhing about like crazed serpents, searching all around.

It was then that it occurred to me the creature probably hadn't spotted us. Maybe it had smelled us or sensed our presence, but it clearly looked like he was searching, like he wasn't quite sure where we were. Then again, maybe he had only sneezed.

The head on the left let out with a long, fiery plume that went high into the sky. Smoke boiled from its nostrils. Then, the beast took a step forward, then another. Wide, leathery wings unfolded, spreading out as big as a basketball court. I had never before seen anything like it . . . not even on television or in the movies! In fact, if I was watching this at a movie theater or reading about it in a book, it might be kind of cool.

But actually being here, live, in person, not only watching, but *experiencing* it . . . well, it wasn't cool at all. It was *terrifying*.

The dragon head on the right let out with a fiery blast, this one going up over our heads, but close enough for us to feel the heat. I was hoping it didn't see us, that it *wouldn't* see us, that it would just rise into the air on its wings and fly off. With the way our luck was going, however, I knew that probably wouldn't happen.

But it *did*.

I couldn't believe it, but the beast turned, crouched down, spread its wings, and, in a loud thunder of flapping, became airborne! In seconds it was soaring up into the sky, higher and higher.

It was the break we needed.

"Let's go!" I shouted to Jason. "I'll bet the Sword of Eternal Power is in there!"

We leapt to our feet and ran toward the cave. I kept glancing up, making sure the dragon wasn't coming back. Thankfully, he was climbing higher and higher into the sky.

We reached the cave. It was even bigger than I imagined! Of course, it had to be, to be the home of such a big creature. If the dragon lived on earth, in our realm, it would easily be the largest living creature on the planet . . . ten times bigger than any whale or elephant.

"We've got to find the sword!" I exclaimed, and my voice echoed, bouncing from wall to wall. "We've got to find it before he comes back!"

We ran frantically around the cave, searching. Oddly, there was nothing in the cave that seemed extraordinary. The ground was a greenish-brown sand, and the walls were made of gray rock.

But as we made our way into the cave, we noticed a faint light farther on. There appeared to be something glowing ahead of us.

"Maybe that's it," Jason said, and the two of us broke into a sprint. As we approached, we realized that it was the glass tomb Dori had told us about! The glass itself seemed to glow on its own, as there was no other source of light!

"I'll bet you're right!" I said to Jason. "That has to be where the sword is!"

But there were two very big problems.

One, we could plainly see the sword was missing.

And two, we could clearly hear the thunder of flapping wings. We spun . . . only to see an enormous shadow darkening the mouth of the cave.

Dantar had returned . . . and we were in his home! He was blocking our only way out!

37

We figured we were doomed.

Without the sword, without anywhere to run, the two-headed dragon would certainly discover us, and we'd be roasted like campfire marshmallows.

Suddenly, one of its heads appeared, glaring at us like an angry school principal. There was no doubt he had spotted us, that was for sure. His huge red eyes looked menacingly at us, and dark smoke drifted from each nostril.

Then, the other head appeared, and the two heads nearly filled the entire cave. They were still some distance away, but if one—or both—of the dragons blew fire in our direction . . . .

I didn't want to think about it.

I glanced all around, looking for some other means of escape. I looked behind me, I looked up and down.

There!

I saw what appeared to be a small hole in the wall of the cave, on the other side of the glass tomb! It certainly wasn't big enough for Dantar to fit through, but Jason and I could.

But it was too late. I wouldn't have time to make it there if I tried.

I had never been so scared in my entire life. I knew that we were never going to make it home again, to earth, to our realm. We'd come this far . . . only to fail. We failed ourselves, and we failed Dori. Maybe even our entire world.

The dragon head on the right sniffed the air. Then, a long, black puff of smoke came out of its nostrils.

Then, its head drew back.

Its mouth opened.

The other dragon head did the same, and I realized what was about to happen.

Both dragon heads were about to attack. Both

of them were only seconds away from sending a searing hot plume of flame into the cave. We weren't going to be cooked by just *one* dragon, but *two*. The dragon, after all, had two heads. Two tornados of fire were about to be unleashed.

I fell to my knees and curled into a ball, giving up all hope. There was nothing I could do.

The two heads began to move. They lunged, and I heard a sudden, piercing roar—

—and then everything went black.

38

Shouting.

That's what I heard. It was a familiar voice, I was sure, calling my name.

Where was I? What had happened? Who was calling my name?

My eyes were closed, and I opened them. I was on the ground, and my surroundings were dim and murky. It was like I was in a cave, or something.

Then, my memories began coming back to me. Dantar, the two-headed dragon—

"Damon!"

—the fire—

"Damon!"

—Jason—

"Damon! You've got to get up! You've got to run!"

Then, I remembered everything: traveling to this strange world; the long, worm-like creatures that attacked us; the weird bird creature that tried to feed us to its babies—

"Damon! Do you hear me?!?!"

—Jason being at my side when the two-headed dragon attacked! But it wasn't Jason's voice that was yelling! It was—

"Don't make me come in there and get you!"

—Kamryn! It was impossible . . . but that's who it was!

I rolled to my knees and stood. The two-headed dragon no longer filled the entrance of the cave. Instead, there was a single person, a girl, who looked tiny compared to the massive opening of the cave.

And in her right arm, she held a sword high, pointed toward the sky. Its blade was glowing brilliantly.

"Kamyrn?!?!" I gasped. "Is . . . is that *you*?!?!"

"Of course it's me!" she shouted. "But hurry!"

I looked around, searching.

"Where's Jason?!?!" I shouted.

"He's already out here! Come on! Hurry!" she glanced nervously over her shoulder, and then she spun. Then, an amazing thing happened. A shadow suddenly fell over her, and a dragon head appeared. While I looked on, Kamryn thrust the sword up into the air. There was an enormous thunderclap, and a bolt of white light shot forth from the sword. The dragon let out a terrible screech, and vanished from view.

Then, Kamryn turned back to me. *"Hurry!"* she ordered again. *"We don't have much time!"*

I sprang, running as fast as I could across the dirt floor of the cave. Kamryn watched me, but kept turning around, eyeing the sky, prepared to defend herself and us.

When I reached the mouth of the cave, I slowed. Then, I stopped near Kamryn.

"I thought you were dead!" I exclaimed.

"I thought I was, too!" she replied. "But I'll tell you about it later! This way!"

I followed her around a large boulder, but a sudden screech in the sky made us both stop and look up. It was Dantar, preparing for another strike. His giant wings beat the air like rolling thunder. He was angry, and he wasn't going to give up easily.

"Go!" Kamryn ordered. She held the sword high

and glanced up at the beast raging in the air above us. "Go to the other side of that big rock over there. I'll take care of him!"

I did exactly what Kamryn ordered . . . realizing too late that, once again, my troubles weren't over.

On the other side of the boulder something was waiting for me:

A huge Night Dragon!

39

I stopped so quickly that I lost my balance and nearly fell forward. Before me, not ten feet away, the black dragon was seated on his hind legs. His wings were folded to his sides and his mouth was open, exposing his long, white teeth. A forked red tongue lolled back and forth, and smoke dribbled from his nostrils.

Why would Kamryn lead me right to a Night Dragon?!?! I thought.

The answer, of course, was that she *wouldn't*. She wouldn't save me, only to put me in harm's way. And in the next moment, I had my answer.

"Don't be afraid!" the black dragon said. "I am from the Emerald Realm! Watch!"

Suddenly, the dragon turned green!

"You see?" he said. "This color is just a disguise. I can change into any color I want. This is how I was able to come to the Realm of Darkness unnoticed by other Night Dragons!"

It was then that Jason appeared. He had been on the other side of the dragon the entire time, scrambling up his back side. Now he appeared, climbing up to the dragon's neck.

"Come on, Damon!" Jason urged, waving me toward him. "We don't have any other choice but to trust him!"

"But what about Kamryn?!?!" I shouted. I turned and caught a glimpse of her. She was wielding the sword with both hands, waving it in front of her like a warrior. Above, the ferocious, two-headed dragon circled, spitting fire and smoke. The creature looked afraid of Kamryn. Oh, he seemed to be plenty mad, all right . . . but it looked as if he didn't want to get too close to her, now that she had the sword.

Suddenly, a fiery bolt of lightning shot from the sword like a jagged laser beam! There was a simultaneous thunderclap that sounded like a canon going off, and the ground shook beneath my feet as the powerful jolt seared into the sky.

Dantar, however, knew what to do. His heads reared back in preparation, then they shot forward as flames spewed from both mouths. The laser beam Kamryn had hurled from the sword stopped, disintegrating in the air before it could reach the dragon.

"Come on!" Jason urged furiously.

"But what about Kamryn?!?!" I repeated.

"She'll be fine! Just climb up!"

I was confused about what had happened and what was going on, but I had to trust Kamryn and Jason . . . and the dragon who said he had come to rescue us. I sprang and ran to the black beast, where Jason helped to pull me up onto its back.

The creature spread its mighty wings and we were suddenly airborne, flying away from the deadly battle between Kamryn and Dantar.

But we didn't go very far. With Jason in front of me, we soared high into the sky, circling far above Dantar. Far below, Kamryn looked like a tiny speck on the ground. Neither she nor the enormous two-headed dragon were paying any attention to us, as they were too busy battling each other.

Wind rushed at my ears. "What happened?" I shouted to Jason.

"I think you fainted," Jason replied loudly. "Just before Dantar tried to cook us, he made a loud roar and backed away. Then, he was gone, and I saw Kamryn with the sword."

How did she get the sword? I wondered.

The dragon we were riding turned to the left. We looked down as Kamryn shot another bolt of white lightning from the sword. Again, Dantar expertly dodged the onslaught and let out with a blast of flame from both of his mouths. I couldn't see Kamryn for a moment, but as the flames went away, I could see she was still safely on the ground, wielding the Sword of Eternal Power.

Jason continued. "She ordered me to get out of the cave and to climb onto the dragon. I wanted to get you first, but she said she would take care of you. I didn't even have time to ask her what happened or how she got the sword."

The dragon we were riding spoke. "Your friend found the sword by accidentally falling into Dantar's lair. She was able to take it while he was gone. I was on my way to help when I found her, and the sword, not far from Dantar's cave. At first, she thought I was a Night Dragon, until I showed her my true color. Then, she knew I was here to help."

"But . . . who are you, then?" I asked.

"I am Samson," the dragon replied. "I was able to disguise myself as a Night Dragon by changing my color and entering the Realm of Darkness. Even if Dantar saw me, he would think I was part of his army. Your friend, it seems, found the sword by mere chance . . . and now, for the first time in thousands of years, we have a chance to defeat Dantar once and for all."

"Not so fast," Jason said. He pointed, and my jaw fell.

On the horizon, I saw a familiar black cloud, moving quickly toward us. A chill shook my entire body.

An army of Night Dragons was coming!

40

"We've got to do something!" I shouted.

Below us, Kamryn was battling with the two-headed dragon. The giant beast kept swooping down at her, but, so far, she was able to resist his attack by using the Sword of Eternal Power. There was fire and smoke and flashes of light all around. The dragon screeched and snarled, and there were loud booms as Kamryn defended herself with the sword. Finally, Dantar landed on the ground. Even from the sky, we could hear the heavy weight of his body on the earth. Flames flew continuously from both mouths as he began storming toward Kamryn, who was still bravely wielding the sword in front of her.

But now there was an army of Night Dragons coming. Kamryn was holding her ground, but only for the time being. There was no way she or we could fight off thousands of angry dragons!

"I have an idea!" Samson growled as he made a swooping turn. "If we can divert the attention of Dantar, that may give your friend a chance to strike with the sword!"

"Yeah, but how are we going to do that?" Jason asked.

"Hold on," Samson said. He folded his wings to his sides. Suddenly, we were plummeting toward the ground like a missile. I had to wrap my arms around Jason's waist to keep from falling off the dragon. Jason, too, had to tighten his arms around the dragon's neck, and it occurred to me that if he fell, I was going to fall, too!

Faster and faster we dove . . . and Samson was aiming right for Dantar!

"I hope he knows what he's doing!" I shouted to Jason as the wind roared past my ears like a hurricane.

"Me, too!" Jason yelled back.

It was all very scary. We were going very, very fast, and in another few seconds, I was sure we were going to slam right into the two-headed dragon.

But it didn't happen.

Samson stretched his wingtips, and we slowed a little bit. Not much, but a little. And by now, we were almost upon Dantar.

Suddenly, he spread his wings to their full extent and let out with a trumpeting, snarling screech. One of Dantar's heads beneath us turned to look up, surprised . . . and that gave Kamryn the time she needed.

Just as Dantar was about to send a plume of fire at us, a bright bolt tore through the sky . . . hitting the two-headed beast square in the chest!

Then, Samson turned, and we were quickly flying out of harm's way. I shot a glance below us . . . and what I saw was *amazing*.

41

Dantar had turned to stone!

Just seconds before, he had been a menacing beast, capable of cooking anything in his path. Now, he looked like a giant statue, carved of dark blue stone.

Harmless.

Kamryn stood on the ground. Her clothing was blackened and her hair was a mess, and she was still holding the sword high above her head, war-like.

Samson wheeled back around, soaring on his mighty wings. We circled, and came to a landing not far from Kamryn.

"Let's get out of here!" I shouted, and Kamryn didn't waste any time. Still wielding the sword, she ran up to Samson, where I grabbed her free hand and helped her onto the dragon's back. When she was seated behind me, Samson spread his wings.

"Ready?" he asked, turning his head.

"Go!" Jason, exclaimed.

We were suddenly airborne again, seated on Samson's powerful back . . . but we weren't out of danger just yet. Behind us, coming fast, was the army of black Night Dragons. I could make out their shapes, their beating wings, even the anger in their faces. Smoke billowed from their nostrils, and several of the beasts blew torrents of yellow fire.

"You must hang on very tight!" Samson growled, and I tightened my grip around Jason's waist. Likewise, Kamryn tightened her grip around mine, while still holding the sword in her free hand.

"If any Night Dragons get close, use the sword!" Samson ordered.

"Oh, believe me, I will!" Kamryn replied loudly.

Suddenly, Samson let out with a burst of speed. The air whooshing by was deafening! Jason shouted something, but his voice was drowned out by the raging wind. I was sure we were going as fast as a jet airplane!

Behind us, the cloud of dragons were still after us. I couldn't tell if we were going faster than they were, though. For our sake, I hoped we were!

Far below, I could see the strange, snake-like creatures rising from their caves and holes. Thankfully, we were so high in the air that they didn't even come close to us.

"Are we going to go back up through that weird, tornado-like thing?!?!" I shouted to Samson.

He turned his head slightly as he replied. "No. That is only an entrance. We must leave this realm by another exit. It is very much like the entrance, except it spirals in the opposite direction. Also, I must warn you: it is much more dangerous."

I didn't know what Samson meant . . . but in seconds, I was about to find out.

Behind us, I could see we were putting more and more distance between us and the army of Night Dragons. What a relief! There must have been thousands of those awful creatures. We'd never be able to fend all of them off!

But what was appearing before us was just as frightening: in the sky was a spinning mass of clouds, much like a hurricane. In fact, it looked oddly similar to the churning whirlpool that we came through to enter into the Realm of Darkness, only now, the mass was above us. The clouds were dark, too, like a huge, rotating thunderstorm.

"This will be difficult," Samson huffed as we raced closer and closer to the spinning vortex. "You'll all have to hold on tight! Whatever you do, don't let go!"

In front of me, Jason had already wrapped both his arms around Samson's neck. I clung tightly to his waist, while Kamryn had one arm clenched around my waist, carrying the sword in her other hand.

And as we drew closer to the cloud, our flight became very bumpy. We jerked this way and that, up and down and all around.

"Almost there!" Samson shouted. "Hang on! We're about to be pulled through!"

Samson wasn't kidding, either! It felt like we were being pulled into a vacuum, sucked up into the mass of whirling clouds.

And it was becoming harder and harder to hold on. The wind was knocking us all over the place, and I could feel Kamryn losing her grip around my waist. Instantly, I grabbed her wrist with my right hand, keeping my left arm looped around Jason.

Kamryn yelled something, but the wind was so loud in my ears I couldn't hear what she'd said.

"Here we go!" Samson growled. Suddenly, he turned upward, and we were headed straight up into the mass of clouds. My grip on Kamryn's wrist was slipping, and I squeezed harder, knowing I couldn't let her go.

But the vacuum proved to be too strong. We were sailing into the clouds at the speed of a rocket, holding on with everything we had . . . but it wasn't enough. I heard Jason's muffled cry, and in the next instant, he no longer had a grip around Samson's neck!

Which meant—

The three of us . . . Jason, Kamryn, and myself . . . were suddenly hurdling through the sky, being pulled higher and higher, faster and faster. We were tumbling so much I could no longer see Samson . . . just the spinning arms and legs of Kamryn and Jason. We were screaming and yelling, confused, and frightened. Terrified, in fact, as we had no idea what was going to happen. All we knew was that we were in big trouble.

Kamryn was shouting something, but I could only make out bits and pieces of her voice. The violent wind was pushing and pulling at us. I became very disoriented, not knowing which way was up or down.

Without warning, Jason was pulled from my grip. A second later, a strong gust of wind yanked Kamryn's wrist from my hand.

I screamed, but there was no one around to

hear. Even *I* couldn't hear myself very well, because the wind was like a roaring freight train!

The clouds around me grew thicker and more dense. Light was fading fast, like a rapidly-approaching nightfall. I caught a glimpse of Kamryn as the wind pulled her farther and farther away from me. She was still carrying the sword, but she was flailing about, out of control.

It grew darker and darker, until I was engulfed in inky blackness. I could see nothing. The only sensation I felt was being pulled, and the wind racing past, knocking me around, causing me to tumble and turn.

This is it, I thought. *This is where it ends.*

And just when I thought there was no hope, an unbelievable thing happened . . . .

43

Suddenly, the darkness was pushed away by daylight! I was still flying upward, toward the sky, but now it felt as if I were being pushed, not pulled. And I was slowing, too.

I could see Kamryn and Jason, not far away. When I looked down, I saw dark, swirling clouds and violent flashes of lightning. In the middle was a dark hole, like the eye of a hurricane.

That's where we came from! I thought. *It sucked us up and spit us out!*

But what was going to happen now? Were we

going to fall back down into the very same hole? Maybe we'd be trapped in the sky forever, being pushed and pulled by the strong currents of air.

Or, maybe we would fall to the ground somewhere, or be sucked into yet another realm. After all, Dori had said thousands of other realms existed.

I shouldn't have worried. I heard a loud screech in the distance, but I couldn't see where it came from. I struggled to turn, but it was hard to do while I was in the air. But I did notice a familiar reddish-orange sky, and I was hopeful that we had returned to the Emerald Realm.

Then, I was no longer being pushed upward. I began falling, descending back to earth . . . or whatever was below us.

And then I saw them: dragons.

Dragons!

There were dozens of them, all different sizes and colors! All of them were flying toward us! They had been waiting for us all along!

Below me, one of the dragons swooped beneath Kamryn, expertly catching her on its back. Kamryn struggled for balance, but finally succeeded in wrapping her legs around the creature and scooping her free arm around the dragon's neck, all the while carefully holding the sword in one hand . . . which was a feat in itself. I couldn't believe she hadn't dropped it.

Instantly, a red dragon was beneath me. It caught me by surprise and I almost fell, but I managed to hold on long enough to pull my legs up and over his back. Then, I wrapped both arms around the dragon's neck and held on tightly.

Meanwhile, Jason, too, had been rescued by a green dragon. The creatures created a formation, and we sailed through the air like a flock of birds. Beneath us, there was nothing to see but dark clouds.

Both Kamryn and Jason were too far away for us to talk to each other. Jason tried yelling to me, but I couldn't understand what he was saying.

And so, we flew on. I tried speaking to the dragon I was riding, but he didn't say anything. Maybe some dragons couldn't talk.

Finally, mountains came into view, and I was certain that we were now back in the Emerald Realm. The clouds beneath us gave way to a rocky ground, and the flock of dragons began to glide downward, around majestic mountains, and over deep, colorful valleys.

Then, we were slowing, cruising not far from the earth's surface. I noticed that in the side of the mountains, there were dozens of caves. Some were at ground level, some were high up. There were dragons in some of the caves, too, and I saw one from our flock actually land at the edge of a cave, where it turned around and sat, watching. Several other dragons did this.

The dragon I was riding on, however, landed on the ground. I slipped from his back, and it occurred to me that riding a dragon was probably a lot like riding a horse . . . a horse with wings, that is.

Not far away, the dragons carrying Jason and Kamryn landed. They each slipped from the dragon they had been riding. Kamryn was mindful of the sword she was carrying, being careful with its blade and keeping the tip pointed toward the ground.

I ran up to them, forgetting all about thanking the red dragon for saving my life. I was just so glad to see Jason and Kamryn alive!

"We did it!" I hollered as I ran up to them. "We stopped Dantar!"

"It's over," Jason said, raising his fist into the air in victory. "It's finally over."

Jason, however, was wrong. Our ordeal wasn't over, for we still had to return to our own realm, to Bismarck, North Dakota, to our homes and families.

And that was going to be another matter altogether.

44

We spent some time with Dori and many other dragons of all shapes and colors. Some, like Dori, changed into their human forms. There were even dragons who changed into kids that could've been my age! I wanted to stay and talk more, but I knew we had to get home . . . and soon.

Still, Dori took the time to answer a few of our questions. We asked what would happen to the Realm of Darkness, now that Dantar had been defeated.

"The Realm of Darkness will always exist," she explained, "and it will always be filled with Night

Dragons and other vile creatures. And," she cautioned, "there is still a chance that Night Dragons could enter into your realm, through Bismarck, where you live. But now that we have the Sword of Eternal Power, it's not very likely to happen. I think most of the Night Dragons will remain where they are, within the Realm of Darkness."

"Will we see you again?" Kamryn asked.

Dori shook her head and smiled. "No, I don't believe you will," she replied. "It is not good to travel among so many different realms. And now that we have the sword safely in our possession, it will no longer be necessary. You helped us a great deal, and we will always remember your courage."

Jason pointed at Kamryn. "She's the one who did it," he said.

Kamryn blushed. "I didn't do anything that anyone else wouldn't have done," she said. "I was just lucky enough to find that tree with the hole inside of it." She explained that she had fallen a long way, only to land on a soft surface, like we had done when we entered the Realm of Darkness.

"It was really dark, and I was scared," she said. "But I saw a light coming from what looked like a tunnel. That tunnel happened to lead right into the back of Dantar's cave."

"I saw that!" I exclaimed. "When Jason and I found where the sword was kept, Dantar returned. We were looking for some way to escape. I saw the tunnel, but I knew we wouldn't make it in time!"

Kamryn continued. "I saw the sword on a small stone table surrounded by glass. Dantar was gone, so I grabbed the sword and ran back into the tunnel. I knew I was safe there, because the tunnel was too small for Dantar to go into. The sword gave off light, so I was able to see as I walked. I guess I got a little lost, but I found another tunnel and followed it, and it led me out to the side of the mountain. Then, Samson found me, and he flew me back to Dantar's cave . . . and just in time! Both his heads looked like they were about to let loose with a blast of fire. All I did was point the sword at him, and WHAM! A jolt of lightning or something came from the blade. I missed Dantar that time, but I sure got his attention."

"That's how you saved us!" I exclaimed. "He was just about ready to cook us, but you got there just in time! If it would have taken you one more second, Jason and I would have been cooked!"

"I just got lucky," Kamryn said. "We all did."

"No," Dori said, "it wasn't luck. You worked hard, and you defeated Dantar. We are forever grateful."

"But how do we get back to our own realm?" I asked.

"It will be easy, now that we have both the Orb of Shammar and the Sword of Eternal Power," Dori replied. Then, looking at Kamryn, she said: "Place the sword into the ground so that it will stand on its own."

Kamryn did as she was asked, and released her grip on the sword handle. Then, she took a step back.

Dori held out her hand. She was holding the Orb of Shammar. She walked toward the sword, held the orb into the air for a moment, and let it go.

It fell . . . but only a few inches. Once again, we watched as it hovered in the air. Only this time, it began to get bigger and bigger—much bigger than it originally had been.

Plus, it took on a filmy, clear look, like plastic. It looked thinner, like we could actually see through it. The orb soon encompassed the sword, and we could actually see the blade and the handle within the growing, dark sphere.

"Step inside the orb," Dori said, and I looked at her like she was crazy. She saw my look of shock and smiled. "You will be all right," she said reassuringly. "The Orb of Shammar will return you safely to you realm. Do you remember our talk about electricity?"

The three of us nodded.

"That is what is going to happen," Dori continued. "The orb will use the energy from the Sword of Eternal Power to safely return you to your realm. Do not be afraid, despite what you see or feel. Now . . . step into the orb. You will find that you will pass right through its skin. And know that we will never forget your bravery."

I was the first to take a step. True to Dori's words, my foot went right through the shimmering orb, which was now very large . . . as big as a car. I could still see the sword within, still plunged into the ground.

I took another step. It was a weird feeling, going through the wall of the sphere. It felt a little like I was passing through warm water.

And then I was all the way inside. I could see out just fine, but everything looked darker, like I was looking through very dark sunglasses.

Then, Jason appeared at my side, followed by Kamryn.

"This is really bizarre," Jason said. "It's like we're inside a giant marble."

Beyond the orb, on the outside, we could still see many dragons, along with those who had taken on their human form. It was then that I realized they truly *were* grateful for our help, that, without us, they would never have been able to defeat Dantar and his Night Dragons. Imagine: three kids from Bismarck, North Dakota, saving the universe from an ugly, two-headed dragon!

It was a good feeling.

I raised my hand to wave to Dori and the others, uncertain what to do next. Was there some sort of button we needed to press? How was this thing supposed to work? I was about to speak, to try and ask Dori what we should do next, but—

Suddenly, a blinding flash of light burst forth from the sword in front of us. Kamryn screamed. I think I did, too. I was instantly blinded, and, at that same moment, realized that something had gone horribly, horribly wrong.

45

We were surrounded by white light so bright I had to close my eyes. Even with my eyes closed, I could sense the intensity of the light, and I covered my eyes with my hands.

What had gone wrong? I wondered. *What is happening?*

It was terrible to think that we'd come this far and were almost on our way home, back to our own realm, only to have something happen.

What if we didn't actually go to our realm? What if we accidentally traveled to another realm, instead?

After all . . . Dori had told us there were thousands of realms. What would we do?

"Damon!" Kamryn screeched. "Are you still here?!?!"

"I'm still here!" I shouted back. "Jason?!?! Are you all right?!?!"

"I'm here!" he shouted, and I realized he was right next to me.

Then, there was a loud explosion that thundered in my chest . . . and the light was gone. At least, with my eyes closed, I sensed it was gone.

Slowly, I lowered my hands and opened my eyes.

Darkness.

We'd gone from one extreme to another. Now, we were in complete darkness, and I couldn't see a thing.

Where are we? I wondered. *Are we home?*

I strained to see or hear anything.

"You guys okay?" I asked.

Kamryn and Jason were still at my side, and they replied that they were fine.

"But I don't like the looks of this," Kamryn said.

"Wait a minute!" Jason suddenly exclaimed. "Listen!"

I cupped my ear, listening intently for any

sound. I heard nothing, until—

"I hear it!" Kamryn exclaimed. "I really do!"

"Shhh!" I hissed.

Then, I *did* hear it: a faint buzzing, like a bug.

"Is that a mosquito?" Jason asked.

"No!" I shouted in sudden realization. "It's an airplane! Listen!"

As the three of us continued listening, we could hear other sounds: crickets and a few faint car honks. And after a moment, the darkness began to lift. It started with a tiny white light in the sky. At first, I thought it was the moon. But as the darkness went away more and more, I realized it was a streetlight! I began to recognize familiar homes and trees on our street. We were in the Kurtzner's front yard, near the sidewalk!

"We're home!" I shouted. "We made it! We really did!"

We were so happy we started jumping up and down. I had been so afraid that we'd never make it home, but we'd made it back to our realm, safe and sound.

But how late were we? Had time *really* stopped for us, like Dori had said? Maybe my mom and dad were out looking for me at this very moment. Maybe I'd be grounded until I was Grandpa's age.

I looked at Kamryn and Jason. Kamryn's clothing was covered with black soot and grime, and her face and bare arms were smeared with it. Jason looked the same. I looked down, and I was pretty dirty, too.

"How am I going to explain this to my parents?" I asked. "I mean . . . they'll never believe me if I tell them I traveled to another world and went to war against giant Night Dragons!"

"You don't have to," Kamryn said. "Just tell them the truth."

"What?!?!" Jason exclaimed.

Kamryn put her hands on her hips. "Well," she began, "are you saying we *lie* to our grandparents?" she asked Jason. She looked at me. "Are you going to lie to your mom and dad?"

I shook my head. "No," I said.

"Exactly," Kamryn said. "So . . . tell them the truth. They'll never believe us, anyway. Even all three of us together."

We said our good-byes, and promised to get together in the morning.

And as it turned out, very little time had passed while we had been away. When I walked into the house and glanced at the clock. I wasn't sure how long I'd been gone, but it was just after eight o'clock . . .

only a few minutes after I was supposed to be home.

Mom was in the living room, reading a book. She didn't say anything about me being late. In fact, she took one look at me and, noticing my disheveled appearance, said: "What on earth have you been doing?"

"Oh, just an ordinary day, Mom," I replied. "You know . . . fighting dragons and stuff. Nothing new."

"Well, get out of those clothes and into the shower. You're filthy. Hope you took care of those dragons." She shook her head.

"Oh, we did," I said . . . and that was the end of it. I was glad to be home, glad to be able to sleep in my own bed, in my own city. I went to bed, thinking about all the things that had happened, thinking that the three of us had experienced the strangest thing anyone in the world had experienced.

In the morning, however, I would find out differently.

I slept in late the next morning. By the time I got up,
Dad had already gone to work, and Mom was in the
living room, watching the morning news on television.

"Strange," she was saying as I poured some
cereal into a bowl.

"What?" I replied with a yawn. I put the cereal
box down and went to the refrigerator. I opened it up
and was about to grab the milk, but Mom's next words
caused me to pause.

"I guess a few people saw and heard some
strange things last night," she said. "Some big flying

things, and some weird noises and lights in the sky."

I paused for another moment, then grabbed the milk and closed the fridge.

"Did you see anything?" Mom asked.

"Just a bunch of fire-breathing dragons," I replied truthfully. "But don't worry. We took care of them. The universe is safe."

"Really, Damon," Mom said with a smirk. "You have a crazy imagination."

"Well, just know that I helped save the world," I said, pouring milk over my cereal. Mom just laughed and kept watching the news. I smiled. Mom and Dad taught me to always tell the truth. I did, and Mom thought I was only kidding. I guess I couldn't blame her.

After breakfast, I went outside. Down the street, I saw Kamryn and Jason sitting on the curb. There was another girl with them, standing partway in the road. Kamryn and Jason appeared to be intensely interested in what the girl was saying.

Jason spotted me and waved me over. I half-jogged across a few lawns and down the sidewalk, stopping at the curb where Kamryn, Jason, and the girl were talking.

Kamryn's eyes grew big. "If you thought what happened to us last night was crazy," she said, "you've got to hear what happened to *her!*"

The girl nodded, and her shiny black hair glimmered in the early morning sun.

"This is Beth Farris," Kamryn said. "She's here visiting relatives, like we are."

"I'm Damon Richards," I said to Beth. Then, I looked at Kamryn and Jason. "Did you tell her what happened to us last night?"

Kamryn and Jason nodded.

"And she believed you?"

"Yeah," Jason said. "Every single word. We told her that she wouldn't, but she says after what happened to her in Montana last week, she'd believe *anything.*"

"What?" I asked. "What happened to you in Montana?"

"Mammoths," Beth said, bobbing her head.

"Mammoths?!?!" I gasped. "But they're extinct!"

"Oh, they're *supposed* to be extinct," Beth replied. "But these mammoths are totally different than any mammoth you've heard of."

"Maybe you should start over," Kamryn said, "so Damon knows the whole story."

"Yeah," I said, squatting down onto the curb. "Let's hear it from the beginning."

"Well, as I was telling Kamryn and Jason . . . my

family went hiking and camping for a week in Montana—and that's how we discovered the horrible mutant mammoths."

As I listened, I knew Beth wasn't making this up. Sure, I'd had a wild adventure with Dori and Dantar and Night Dragons—but Beth Farris had her own horrifying experience . . . with the mutant mammoths of Montana!

NEXT IN THE AMERICAN CHILLERS SERIES:

#20:

MUTANT MAMMOTHS OF MONTANA

Continue on to read sample chapters!

The alarm clock rang, jolting me awake. I slapped at it in the darkness until it stopped, then I fell back onto my pillow.

It was five a.m.

Although my bedroom door was closed, there was a thin band of light coming from beneath it. Mom and Dad were already up and moving about, getting ready for the day, packing our gear.

And I'm exhausted, I thought. *I can't believe I'm getting up this early.*

Oh, don't get me wrong. It was the first day of our camping vacation, and I had been excited for months. Every summer, we go somewhere fun. Last year, we went to Disneyland. The year before that, we went to California, where my cousins live. That's where my brother, Reese, fell and broke his arm.

But this year, we were staying in our home state of Montana. I remember the day Mom and Dad asked me about their idea. They had been talking in the kitchen, then they came to my room and stood at the door. I was on my bed, reading a book, and I put it down and looked at them.

"Beth, what would you think about going on a camping trip this summer?" Mom asked.

"That would be cool!" I exclaimed. "Like . . . in a tent?"

Dad nodded. "Yes," he said. "We'll take two tents, and we'll use them for the whole week."

"And cook food over a fire?" I asked.

Mom and Dad nodded, smiling.

"That would be so much fun!" I exclaimed. "Have you asked Reese?"

"Not yet," Dad said. "But you know *him*. He loves the outdoors. I'm sure he'll be thrilled."

"Where are we going to go?" I asked.

"We haven't decided yet," Mom replied. "We wanted to make sure that you and your brother would want to do it."

"Are you kidding?!?!" I exclaimed as I sat up and placed my feet on the floor. "Camping would be great!"

"Usually, we always stay in hotels," Dad said, "but we thought it might be fun to explore the wilderness, for a change. You know . . . do something different. Go for some hikes and do some exploring. I think it'll be fun, and we'll learn a lot about nature."

From that day forward, all I could think about was our upcoming camping trip. We looked through catalogs and went to sporting good stores to buy equipment. I got a new pair of hiking boots and a new windbreaker, along with a rain parka.

Then, one day, Mom and Dad decided where we were going to go: Glacier National Park.

Glacier National Park! I couldn't believe it! Glacier National Park is world famous! We live in Great Falls, Montana, which is about 130 miles away from the park . . . but we've never been there. Glacier National Park is huge: it has more than 700 miles of trails, and is home to mountain goats, cougars, grizzly bears, and lots of other animals.

It also has 27 glaciers, but they are melting fast. Dad says that he read in the news that in thirty or forty years, all the glaciers will probably have melted away.

I was really excited to camp at Glacier, but I was a little nervous . . . and maybe even a little scared.

Cougars? I thought. *Grizzly bears?*

While I thought it might be cool to see them, I wouldn't want to see them up close!

I needn't have worried. Cougars and grizzly bears were going to be the least of our troubles. Our troubles were going to be much bigger than that.

Several *tons* bigger, as a matter of fact.

After a few minutes of laying in bed and listening to the sounds of my mom and dad scurrying around the house, I sat up. My bedroom door opened, and light flooded in. The dark silhouette of my mom appeared.

"Rise and shine," she said, as I raised my arm to cover my eyes from the harsh light that swamped my room.

I smiled thinly. "I'm awake," I replied.

"We'll be leaving at six," Mom said. "Double check you gear, and make sure you have everything you need." She walked away, and I could hear shuffling around the house as she and Dad continued getting ready for our trip.

Too cool, I thought as I scrambled out of bed. I didn't think this day was ever going to get here.

After wolfing down a quick bowl of cereal, I went back to my room. I had made a list of all the things to take, but most of the stuff was already packed. The only things I needed to get were things like toothpaste and soap.

Our plan was this: we would drive from our home in Great Falls to Glacier National Park. Dad said the trip would take us a couple of hours. From there, we would drive deep into the park to a place called Kintla Lake Campground. Kintla Lake Campground is located deep in the park, way up in the northwest corner in an area known as North Fork. Dad showed me the brochure. It was small; there were only about a dozen campsites, and the camping area was on the shores of Kintla Lake. Dad said that because it is so remote, there probably wouldn't be too many other campers. But not far away was a small community called Polebridge, so if we needed supplies, we could go there.

At Kintla Lake Campground, we would set up our tents, and it would be our 'home base' for the entire week. From there, we would hike, fish, and explore. With so many miles of miles of hiking trails, there would be plenty of things to do, and plenty of things to see. Maybe even a grizzly bear.

So, you can imagine how excited I was. I was ready for seven whole days of adventure.

Our seven-day adventure, however, wasn't going to be anything like we thought. Sure, it would be filled with a lot of adventure.

But it would also be filled with something else:

Terror.

3

The trip from Great Falls to Glacier was boring. We drove our van, which has a lot of room inside. Even with all of our camping gear, I could still recline in my seat and stretch out. I fell asleep for a little while, but I woke up when Reese started poking me in the ribs. We got into an argument, but he was the one who started it. He always starts arguments. I never do. But he got into trouble for calling me a boogerhead, and Mom made him leave me alone. Then I asleep again.

    I was awakened by bright sunlight coming through the van window. I sat up and used my arm to shade my face. Outside, the van moved along a paved road. Trees and mountains rose into a perfect, blue sky. There were no other cars around.

Reese had fallen asleep in his seat. At some point, he'd eaten a chocolate bar, and he had a dab of brown goo around the edges of his mouth. He looked silly.

Mom was in the front passenger seat, and she turned. "Have a nice nap?" she asked.

"Yeah," I said with a yawn. "Where are we?"

"We're in the park already," Mom explained.

Holy cow, I thought. I've slept nearly the entire trip!

"So, how far are we from Kintla Lake Campground?" I asked.

"We still have a little ways to go," Dad replied. "We'll have to travel some bumpy roads to get there, so get ready."

While Reese slept, I turned and looked out the window. Everything was so scenic and beautiful, and I thought about all of the things we would do over the next seven days. I had a new digital camera that was a birthday gift from Mom and Dad, so I planned on taking a lot of pictures.

Soon, we were on a rugged, dirt road. The van

bounced all around, waking Reese. When he first woke up, he looked silly. He was groggy, and he still had chocolate goo around his mouth. He didn't know it, though, and I wasn't going to tell him.

"Where . . . where are we?" he stammered as he balled his fists and rubbed his eyes.

"We're almost home," I teased. "They don't allow goofy boys at the park, so we had to take you back."

Reese didn't say anything. Instead, he stuck his tongue out at me.

Typical Reese, I thought, turning to look out my window.

At that very moment, I saw something at the edge of the forest. At first, I couldn't believe it.

I wouldn't believe it.

I was looking at a monster!

At first, I thought I was looking at a rock formation. As we bounced along the road, the trees were set back a little, and there were some big rocks and boulders nestled along the edge of the forest. Behind and above the trees, larger, jagged mountains loomed.

But a certain large boulder (at least, that's what I thought it was, at first) looked out of place.

Like it didn't belong.

And then I could make out a mouth.

And eyes.

I could see two long tusks, like a bull elephant, and enormous ears. The thing was covered with thick, gray fur that was matted and dirty.

And its legs were gigantic, the size of tree trunks! They, too, looked liked elephant legs, except they appeared to have claws like that of a bear. But it was no elephant, that was for sure. And besides: what would an elephant be doing in Montana?

Suddenly, we went around a bend in the road, and I could no longer see the creature.

"Did . . . did anyone else see that?!?!" I blurted.

"See what?" Mom asked.

"Dad, stop!" I said. "I saw something back there!"

"What?" Dad asked.

"I don't know!" I said. "But it looked like an elephant . . . except it was bigger and uglier!"

This brought a round of laughter from everyone: Mom, Dad, and Reese.

"Bigger and uglier?" Reese said. "That was just your reflection in the window."

I ignored him. "No, really!" I pleaded. "There was some big animal back there! I saw it with my own eyes!"

"You boogerhead," Reese hissed quietly, so Mom and Dad wouldn't hear.

"There aren't any animals in the park that big," Mom said. "Maybe it was a moose."

"I know a moose when I see one," I said, and it was true. We have moose in Montana, and I see them once in a while.

I turned all the way around in my seat, straining against the seatbelt. I was hoping to get another glimpse of whatever it was . . . but we were too far away, and there were too many trees.

Maybe it was just my imagination, I thought. Maybe it was nothing. After all . . . I just woke up. Maybe I'm still sleepy.

And that's what I told myself. I told myself that I had imagined the strange creature at the edge of the forest. I told myself that Mom was right: there aren't any animals that big in Glacier National Park. In fact, there aren't animals that big anywhere in America . . . except in zoos and circuses.

I wouldn't be telling myself that for long. Soon, we'd know the truth . . . and our camping trip to Glacier National Park was going to turn into a fight for our lives!

FUN FACTS ABOUT NORTH DAKOTA:

State Capitol: Bismarck

State Fossil: Teredo Petrified Wood

State Nickname: Peace Garden State

State Beverage: Milk

State Bird: Western Meadowlark

State Fish: Northern Pike

State Tree: American Elm

State Grass: Western Wheatgrass

State Flower: Wild Prairie Rose

Statehood: November 2nd, 1889 (39th state)

FAMOUS NORTH DAKOTANS!

Louis L'Amour, author

Lawrence Welk, band leader

Peggy Lee, singer

Angie Dickinson, actress

Eric Sevareid, TV commentator

Ivan Dmitri, artist

Larry Woiwode, writer

James Renquist, painter

Harold K. Johnson, army general

Phil D. Jackson, basketball player, coach

among many, many more!

ABOUT THE AUTHOR

Johnathan Rand is the author of more than 50 books, with well over 2 million copies in print. Series include **AMERICAN CHILLERS, MICHIGAN CHILLERS, FREDDIE FERNORTNER, FEARLESS FIRST GRADER**, and **THE ADVENTURE CLUB.** He's also co-authored a novel for teens (with Christopher Knight) entitled **PANDEMIA.** When not traveling, Rand lives in northern Michigan with his wife and two dogs. He is also the only author in the world to have a store that sells only his works: **CHILLERMANIA!** is located in Indian River, Michigan. Johnathan Rand is not always at the store, but he has been known to drop by frequently. Find out more at:

www.americanchillers.com

JOIN THE FREE AMERICAN CHILLERS FAN CLUB!

It's easy to join . . . and best of all, it's FREE!
Find out more today by visiting:

WWW.AMERICANCHILLERS.COM

And don't forget to browse the on-line superstore, where you can order books, hats, shirts, and lots more cool stuff!

Johnathan Rand travels internationally for school visits and book signings! For booking information, call:

1 (231) 238-0338!